RUNNING OUT OF TIME

"You mean you think if we get Samson to tolerate the stirrups Max will let him stay?" Lisa asked.

"Definitely. I'm sure that's why he suddenly decided to send him to a trainer—he thinks we can't solve this problem." Carole stood to hang up the bridle she'd been oiling. "Luckily, Max is going to be at that dressage show, so we'll have plenty of time."

Lisa nodded thoughtfully. "I guess it can't hurt."

"Can't hurt? It's our only chance to keep Samson here," Carole replied.

"Okay, then," Lisa said after a minute, "count me in."

THE SADDLE CLUB

PLEASURE HORSE

BONNIE BRYANT

A SKYLARK BOOK
NEW YORK • TORONTO • LONDON • SYDNEY • AUCKLAND

RL 5, 009–012

PLEASURE HORSE
A Skylark Book / February 1996

ISBN 0-553-48269-6

Published simultaneously in the United States and Canada

Bantam Books are published by Bantam Books, a division of Bantam Dou-
bleday Dell Publishing Group, Inc. Its trademark, consisting of the words
"Bantam Books" and the portrayal of a rooster, is Registered in U.S. Patent
and Trademark Office and in other countries. Marca Registrada. Bantam
Books, 1540 Broadway, New York, New York 10036.

PRINTED IN THE UNITED STATES OF AMERICA
OPM   0 9 8 7 6 5 4 3 2

*I would like to express my special
thanks to Caitlin Macy for her
help in the writing of this book.*

PLEASURE HORSE

"I'D BETTER GET OFF before I *fall* off!" Stevie Lake exclaimed. She hopped to the ground and shook her finger reprovingly at Belle, her bay mare. "If I didn't know better, I'd say you hadn't been out of your stall in months!"

"It must be the weather," said Lisa Atwood. "Prancer was just as bad. She spooked at the same corner of the ring nine times!"

"Ditto for Starlight," said Carole Hanson, dismounting to join her two friends. "You'd think by February they'd be used to the sound of the wind blowing

1

outside the indoor ring, but Starlight was as skittish as a colt today."

The girls had just finished their Tuesday-afternoon riding lesson at Pine Hollow Stables and, as usual, were heading into the barn together to untack. Besides taking lessons in the same group, Carole, Lisa, and Stevie spent practically every waking hour together.

Since all three of them loved horses, a lot of those hours were spent at Pine Hollow. Stevie and Carole boarded their horses there, and Lisa always rode Prancer, a Thoroughbred stable horse. To make the time there even more fun, the girls had started a club for people who were horse-crazy. It was called The Saddle Club. Besides being horse-crazy, the only other requirement was that members be willing to help each other out in any kind of situation.

"Skittish as a colt?" Lisa repeated Carole's comment. "Hey, speaking of colts, weren't we going to work with Samson today?"

Samson, a coal-black colt, had been bred and born at Pine Hollow. The Saddle Club had been helping out with his training since day one—or even before, since they'd taken care of his mother while she was in foal and had been there at his birth. With all the patient care he had received, it was no wonder that he was maturing into a lovely horse. Of course, his breeding was important, too. Samson was the son of Delilah, an attractive palomino mare that was one of Pine Hollow's best pleasure horses.

Samson's father was Cobalt, a black Thoroughbred. Cobalt had been an amazing jumper until he had broken a leg in a tragic accident caused by his rider's carelessness. Veronica diAngelo, a spoiled, snobby girl who rode at Pine Hollow, had ignored instructions and taken Cobalt over a jump in a dangerous way. The horse had fallen and injured himself so badly there had been no choice but to put him down. Despite missing Cobalt, The Saddle Club was thrilled that Samson seemed to have inherited his sire's spirit, and also his dam's sweet disposition.

"That's right, we are supposed to work with Samson," Carole replied, "and today we're supposed to try the saddle with the stirrups on him."

"Good—that's an important step for him," said Lisa.

The Saddle Club had seen Samson go from wearing a halter for the first time to getting used to a bridle and saddle. They took the task of training the colt very seriously and had made sure to go slowly to avoid upsetting him. So far Samson had only worn a saddle without

3

stirrups, but the girls had decided he was ready for the next step.

"Before long he'll have a rider on his back," Stevie predicted.

"Won't that be incredible?" Lisa cried. "I wonder who will be the first to sit on Samson."

"I'll bet Max will want to do that part himself," said Carole.

Maximillian Regnery III, Max for short, was the owner of Pine Hollow Stables and the girls' riding instructor. He had inherited the farm from his father, who had inherited it from *his* father, usually referred to as Max the First. The current Max was an experienced all-around horseman. If he was the first to ride Samson, there was no doubt that he would do an excellent job.

"Still, maybe if we do our best, he'll consider letting us at least help out on the big day. And then, you never know," Stevie said, her hazel eyes twinkling.

Carole and Lisa grinned. It was much too early to guess who would get to ride the colt first, but with Stevie Lake on their team, it was true: You *did* never know. Stevie had an incredible talent for getting people to do what she wanted. Even though the talent seemed to be inborn, with all the adventures she'd gotten The Saddle Club into and out of, Stevie had found plenty of opportunities to develop it.

"Anyway, let's get him used to the stirrups first, okay?" Lisa suggested.

"Right. How about we untack and meet back in the indoor ring in half an hour?" said Carole. "I'll bring Samson. You guys bring a saddle with stirrups."

The girls agreed and split up.

CAROLE HUMMED AS she groomed Starlight on the cross-ties. She loved fussing over the bay gelding, but today she couldn't wait to work with Samson. He was more than just another horse to Carole. She felt she had a special bond with the colt because she had ridden his sire. Whenever Veronica had been too lazy to exercise Cobalt, Carole had taken the stallion out. For a short time, right before the accident, the two of them had made a great team.

When Cobalt had been put down, Carole had thought she would never ride again. In the end, though, her love of horses had won out. She'd gotten back in the saddle and kept riding. Now she had her own horse, Starlight, whom she adored. But she had never forgotten Cobalt, and it made her extremely proud that she was helping train his son to become as fine a horse as he had been.

After she finished rubbing Starlight down, putting him away, and checking his hay and water, Carole went to Samson's stall. The colt stuck his nose over the door the minute he heard Carole's voice.

"Hey, Mr. Friendly," Carole said, patting the glossy black neck. She snapped a lead line to his halter and led him out into the aisle. Even though he was still at the "awkward stage," with his rump a good hand or two higher than his withers, Samson had the makings of a very handsome horse. His short back, sloping shoulder, and refined head spoke miles about his good breeding, even at this young age.

"All right, I'd better stop admiring you," Carole admitted reluctantly. "I wouldn't want you to get conceited—at least not yet."

Samson playfully nodded his head and danced on the end of the lead line as Carole led him into the indoor ring.

"He looks raring to go," Lisa observed.

"He is full of energy today," Carole agreed.

As they always did, the girls spent a few minutes patting and speaking to the colt. All of the training they had done so far followed the methods of natural horsemanship they'd learned from Denise McCaskill, a college student who sometimes worked at the stables. "Natural" horsemanship meant training by positive encouragement instead of by force, or, as Stevie liked to say, "By the carrot, not the whip." It involved many techniques, including equine massage and voice training. The focus of each training session was supposed to be teaching, not correcting.

"I think I'll take him for a couple of turns around the ring to let him check things out," Carole said.

Even though Samson had seen the indoor ring hundreds of times, Carole knew that it was important to go slowly at every step of the colt's training. Letting him walk around for a while instead of shoving a saddle on him right away would set a relaxed tone for the rest of the lesson.

"We'll go with you," Stevie volunteered. "I wouldn't mind stretching my legs, either."

"Sore from Max's class?" Lisa asked.

Stevie shook her head. "Riding? No way. It's sitting at a desk all day that makes me stiff!"

The girls laughed. Unlike Lisa, who breezed through school and liked it, or Carole, who tolerated it, Stevie maintained an active dislike for all things academic.

"Well, just think," said Lisa, "Presidents' Day is coming up, so there'll be a long weekend soon—three days to stretch your legs instead of two."

Stevie perked up. "I almost forgot about the long weekend. I don't know how on earth, but I did. Actually, that reminds me. We're going to visit my relatives in New Jersey. There's going to be a big party for my cousin Angie's sixteenth birthday. It should be fun."

"What's your cousin like?" Carole asked. "Doesn't she ride?"

"Yeah, she's pretty good. I haven't seen her for a few years, but we've always gotten along well—probably because she's horsey, too. She has her own horse and goes to lots of shows. I'll probably be able to ride while we're up there because my aunt and uncle have horses, too. I guess the only bad part will be that I'll miss a couple of days working with Samson."

"We'll give you a full update when you get back," Carole promised.

By the time they had circled the ring twice, Samson seemed quieter. He pranced when the wind outside picked up and shook the rafters, but otherwise he was calm. Stevie got the saddle from the jump where it was resting and she and Lisa placed it carefully on Samson's back.

"Make sure the stirrups don't hit him," Carole said.

"Don't worry—they're still rolled up. He can't feel a thing," Lisa assured her. She waited while Stevie gently tightened the girth.

"All right, we'll unroll them now. Okay, Carole?" Stevie asked.

Carole nodded. So far the lesson was going perfectly.

Moving quietly, Lisa and Stevie each unrolled one of the stirrups so that the irons hung down below the saddle flaps. Carole was about to ask Samson to walk forward when the colt seemed to realize that something was swinging from the saddle. He shied to the side in surprise.

"Easy, boy, don't get all worked up. It's only a pair of stirrups," Carole said, trying to soothe him. She placed one hand on his neck. Instead of listening to her, Samson threw his head up and danced away.

"Do you think he's frightened by them?" Lisa asked anxiously.

"I—I don't know," Carole admitted. She couldn't say much more because it was taking all her concentration to steady Samson.

"Or maybe it's the wind again. It *is* loud," Lisa suggested. It wasn't like Samson to be so high-strung.

"I don't think he's scared," Stevie observed. "Look at his face. It's more playful than frightened. I'll bet he thinks this whole thing is a big game."

The girls looked. Samson did seem to be playing. By now he was virtually ignoring Carole, pulling and prancing and tossing his head around for emphasis.

"You know, I think you're right. He's like a kitten with a new ball of yarn," Carole remarked, thinking of

9

her cat, Snowball. She had to raise her voice so that the others could hear her, because Samson had pulled her with him as he pranced his way down to the end of the ring.

"Yeah, or a brother trying to beat you in an argument," Stevie muttered, thinking of her three easily incensed siblings.

Speaking firmly and with a couple of snaps on the lead line, Carole managed to get Samson back to the middle of the ring. But once there, he refused to stand still. Stevie and Lisa tried to help, but they weren't sure what to do. When they approached Samson, he shied away; when they stayed back, he started to drag Carole around. Carole kept talking to him quietly and patting him and telling him everything was okay, but Samson didn't seem to be listening. Finally Lisa suggested that they call it quits for the day, even though they'd only been out about ten minutes. "We don't want him to get too excited," she said. "And let's face it: This is becoming a battle that we're losing. He's really out of control."

"I agree. And if he gets any sweatier, it's going to take hours to walk him," Stevie said, noting the wet shine that had quickly appeared on Samson's dark coat. "What do you think, Carole?"

Carole didn't say anything at first, but then she nodded reluctantly. She hated to give up when the lesson had started so well, but she knew that her friends were right. A good horsewoman never continued when a horse got too worked up, especially a young horse. In one very bad session, a trainer could undo a lot of good work.

Together, the three girls could barely get the saddle off. Samson kept lunging away, and it still wasn't clear if he was spooked or just being silly. Exhausted, Carole relinquished the lead line to Stevie so Stevie could walk Samson to cool him off. "I don't understand what I was doing wrong," Carole commented, watching the colt slowly quiet down again.

"I don't think you were doing anything wrong," Lisa said sympathetically. "He was just acting strange. Remember, every horse, trainer, and rider has off days. None of us knew what to do."

Carole nodded thoughtfully. Stevie had reached the end of the ring and turned Samson back toward them. Once again it hit Carole how striking the colt was and how well he would perform under saddle someday. The thought made her feel better. "You're right, Lisa," she said brightly. "I guess I just thought that since he's taken every other step of his training so calmly, this one would be no different. We'll just have to go more slowly with the stirrups if he doesn't like them, that's all."

Overhearing, Stevie brought Samson up to the two of

them. "I agree completely. So far we've had it easy, but training Samson is going to be a challenge, like most things about horses. And since all of our horses are working well for the moment, the three of us could use a little challenge around here."

"Don't say that without knocking wood!" Lisa exclaimed.

"Say what, that we need a challenge?" Stevie asked.

"No! That all of our horses are working well!" Lisa cried.

"All right, now you've both said it. Go knock on those cavalletti while I hold Samson," Carole instructed. Lisa and Stevie ran and rapped on the jumps.

"Satisfied?" Stevie asked.

"With you, yes," Carole replied. She turned to Samson and added, under her breath, "And more determined than ever to keep working with you."

STEVIE GRITTED HER TEETH. By all accounts, she should have been in a great mood. Here it was, the Friday of Presidents' Day weekend. She had three whole days off from school, and she was on the train to visit a cousin who loved horses as much as she did. Unfortunately, her three brothers—Chad, the oldest; her twin, Alex; and Michael—were on the same train. Even more unfortunately, Stevie was stuck in a four-seater with them, all the way from Virginia to Philadelphia, while her parents snoozed in a double seat several rows away. Sometimes Stevie thought that the universe might not be big enough for her and her brothers. But she was absolutely, positively, one-hundred-percent sure that one train seat was far too small.

For a while Stevie had been pretending to be asleep so that she could ignore them, but it wasn't working all that well. With her eyes closed, she only heard every annoying thing they said more clearly. Michael had been humming off-key for the last hour while Chad and Alex discussed all the cute girls they were planning to charm at Angie's sweet sixteen party on Sunday.

"What about Angie's friend, the blond girl we met that time at Christmas?" Alex asked.

"Who? Oh, you mean the one who does ballet?" Chad asked.

"Yeah."

"No problem. She liked me that time we visited them before."

"I don't know . . . I thought she liked me."

"You guys? How does 'I've Been Working on the Railroad' go again?" Michael interrupted.

"Why would she like you?" Chad asked. "I'm older."

"So? What does age have to do with it?"

"You guys! Will you tell me the tune?" Michael demanded. "I can't remember it. I just know, 'Someone's in the kitchen with Dinah,' and then I get all messed up."

With a long-suffering sigh, Stevie sat up in her seat. She opened her eyes and glared until she had her brothers' attention. "Did it ever occur to the three of you that I just might be trying to sleep?" she asked, her voice saccharine.

Chad, Alex, and Michael paused for a millisecond. "No," Alex said. They all burst out laughing.

With a supreme effort, Stevie managed to restrain herself from attacking them with her train pillow. "Ha-ha, aren't you funny, Alex," she said. "I wish I could be that amusing."

"Maybe you could be if you didn't spend eight days a week up to your elbows in horse manure," Alex retorted.

Pretending not to hear, Stevie clamped the pillow over her ears and pressed her head back against the seat. She glanced at her watch: two long hours to go. What could she do to distract herself for *two hours*?

I know, Stevie thought suddenly, *I'll think—really think —about what to do about Samson*. That could take days, it was such a challenging case. If she thought of anything, maybe she could call Carole and Lisa from her cousin's. Or better yet, maybe Angie would even have a suggestion on how to solve the problem. For it had become a problem. Even though The Saddle Club had been working patiently, the colt was no closer to accepting the strange swinging objects than he had been

15

the first time. It was if something snapped in his brain whenever the stirrups came out of the tack room.

Every lesson had gone about the same. First they would walk Samson to relax him. Then they would put the saddle on, hoping for the best. But as soon as the colt was tacked up, whether they had walked him for five minutes beforehand or for almost an hour, he would start to act up. It had gotten to the point where he started dancing around the minute he saw the saddle. The worst thing, Stevie knew, was that she and Lisa and Carole weren't sure how to react. It was hard to know how to discipline a horse from the ground. They were used to *riding* horses that played around, but that didn't seem to be helping.

Still, Stevie hadn't said anything to her friends, mainly because after a bad session with Samson, Carole always looked so dismayed that Stevie didn't have the heart to rub it in. She knew how much it meant to Carole to be the one to train Cobalt's son, and she didn't want to be pessimistic. Besides, there was no doubt in her mind that the three of them *could* do the job. It just might take a little time.

Brooding about Samson, Stevie didn't notice the miles rushing by. Before she knew it, her parents were on their feet telling her and the boys to collect their luggage and prepare to get off the train because it was pulling

16

into Union Station in Philadelphia. Stevie's aunt and uncle lived just over the Pennsylvania border in New Jersey.

"Do we have time to run to the snack car one more time?" Alex asked.

"Absolutely not," said Mrs. Lake. "You've eaten enough junk between D.C. and here to pollute a small swamp. Now, shake a leg—the train is fifteen minutes behind schedule, and Uncle Chester and Aunt Lila will be waiting."

"Hold on! Wait for me—I can't carry all my stuff!" Michael exclaimed.

"What on earth did you pack?" Mr. Lake demanded, grabbing his youngest son's two huge suitcases.

"Just a few things to make me feel at home. My Nintendo Game Boys, my two soldier collections, my stuffed dog . . ."

Stevie smiled. Family vacations were so predictable that, once in a while, it was almost comforting.

The Lakes had barely set foot inside Union Station when they heard their names being called. Uncle Chester, Aunt Lila, and their daughter Angie descended upon them, arms outstretched. Uncle Chester and Stevie's father were brothers. They looked a lot alike except for the fact that Uncle Chester was a little older and had a handlebar mustache. The two men clapped

17

each other on the back while the kids and the mothers greeted one another.

"Angie!"

"Stevie!" The two girls hugged enthusiastically. Then Angie turned to say hi to the boys. Suddenly Stevie noticed that her cousin looked different. Instead of the tomboy Stevie remembered, Angie was stylishly dressed in a short wool skirt and V-neck sweater. She was wearing lipstick, pearl earrings, and a gold headband to hold back her long blond hair.

"Stevie, great to have you here!" Stevie's uncle enveloped her in a bear hug.

Talking a million miles an hour, the two families headed to the lot where the New Jersey Lakes' van was parked. Angie and Stevie fell into step together.

"How's Sparkles?" Stevie asked right away. Sparkles was the nickname of Angie's horse, a well-built palomino whose show name was Spark of Genius. He was talented over fences, and Angie had done well with him in junior jumper classes.

"He's fine—same as always," Angie answered briefly. Then she smiled. "I'm so glad you could make it down for the weekend, Stevie. My party is going to be incredible. Did you know we're having it catered? The food is going to be great—hors d'oeuvres, a buffet supper, and a super-fancy cake for dessert. And we're getting the most

18

gorgeous flowers—not just plain bouquets but special arrangements. The best florist in Philadelphia is doing them."

Stevie nodded absently. Of course the party would be fun, but she could hardly wait to get out to the barn and see the horses. She was planning on taking at least one ride a day with Angie. "So how many horses do you have now? Bones and Birdie are still around, right?" Stevie asked, referring to the Lakes' two hunters. Bones was older and had been semiretired for a few years.

"Oh, sure," Angie said offhandedly. "We'll never get rid of those two."

Stevie was about to ask where Angie wanted to ride first when her cousin gave a little cry of excitement. "I almost forgot! You know what else?" Angie asked.

Stevie shook her head.

Angie beamed. "There's going to be a really cool band from my school. It's a bunch of guys I know. They played at one of my friends' sweet sixteen parties, and they were amazing."

Overhearing, Chad turned to the girls. "Yeah? What kind of music do they play?"

"Everything!" Angie replied. She and Chad began to compare notes on the music and bands they liked. Only half listening, Stevie found her mind straying from the conversation.

19

"So, isn't that going to be great?" Angie said finally.

It took Stevie a minute to realize that her cousin was addressing her. "Yeah, it sounds fun," she answered, hoping that she sounded more enthusiastic than she felt. Somehow Stevie wasn't all that impressed by the party details. But Angie seemed so excited that the only thing Stevie could do was to try to act excited, too.

It was strange, though. In the past, the girls had spent hours riding and fussing over Sparkles, Bones, and Birdie. Now Angie seemed too preoccupied with the party even to talk about the horses.

Stevie decided to have another try. A couple of years ago, the thing Angie had wanted most of all was to compete successfully on the "A" circuit, the highest level of horse showing. Her parents had bought Sparkles, an experienced show horse, to help her accomplish that goal. Stevie vividly remembered Angie vowing to be one of the top junior jumper riders on the east coast by the time she was sixteen. And that was only two days away. "Angie," Stevie began tentatively, "how did you and Sparkles do last season on the show circuit?"

Angie looked surprised by the question. "I haven't been showing him all that much," she replied.

"Really?" Stevie repeated. "But I thought you were planning to—"

Angie interrupted with a loud laugh. "Planning to go

all the way to the American Horse Show, right? I remember. Boy, that seems like a long time ago." With that, Angie once again abruptly changed the subject back to her party. She started to tell Stevie about her choice of dresses: green velvet or black silk.

When the two families reached the van, they all piled in, and Uncle Chester headed for the bridge to New Jersey. Squeezed between Angie and her mother, Stevie resigned herself to listening to more party clothing details. Every few minutes she murmured "Really?" or "Wow" to be polite, although it was hard to feign interest about which shoes would match which dress.

Stevie was surprised that Angie wasn't showing. Sparkles was such a good jumper that he belonged in the show ring. Using him as a pleasure horse was a waste of his talent. Stevie decided to ask Angie about it when they went riding. For now, she could hardly get a word in edgewise.

When they got to the house, Angie showed Stevie to the room she would be staying in. It was a guest room on the second floor, right next to Angie's. "Oh, good—this means I can sneak into your room so we can talk till all hours," Stevie said.

Angie nodded, but she didn't seem thrilled by the prospect. "We can't stay up too late, Stevie. I don't want to look all tired for the party, you know."

21

If her cousin's face had not been so serious, Stevie would have burst out laughing. That was a new one: Angie Lake needing her beauty rest.

"This is really a big-deal party, huh?" Stevie asked.

Angie's face lit up. "It really is. Mom and I have been planning for months."

Stevie dropped her bag, kicked off her shoes, and sprawled on one of the beds. Angie perched carefully on the other one, smoothing her skirt down over her legs. "How's school, Stevie?" Angie inquired.

"Boring, dull, boring, and dull," Stevie replied cheerfully. "How about for you?" One thing she and Angie had always agreed on was that school took way too much time away from riding.

"It's great," Angie said. "All my friends and I have so much fun, you wouldn't believe it." With that, the older girl stood up and walked over to check her hair in the bedroom mirror.

Stevie sighed. *No, I probably wouldn't,* she thought.

"MEET YOU IN the tack room?" Lisa asked.

Carole nodded. "Right. I want to oil those bridles we cleaned yesterday," she said. The two girls had just finished another frustrating training session with Samson. But even though she was dejected, Carole was determined to maintain a positive attitude. One way to do that was to help out at Pine Hollow the way she always did. Right now she felt like crawling home and collapsing on her bed. Instead, she would oil some tack and try to work herself out of her funk.

Samson was cross tied in the main aisle, and Carole

gave him a pat on the neck before leading him back to his stall. By patting him and praising him, Carole made sure that she wasn't holding a grudge against Samson just because things weren't going well. "I know it's not your fault, Samson," Carole murmured, inside the stall. "But can't you just tell me why you don't like stirrups? They're not that bad, you know. Just a couple of pieces of iron. If you don't get used to them, how are you going to become a nice pleasure horse like your mother?"

Samson arched his neck prettily and blew through his nostrils. "All the good looks in the world aren't going to get you anywhere if nobody can ride you," Carole informed him. Reluctantly, she gave the colt a final pat and closed and bolted his stall door.

"I'd say today went a little better," Lisa said as Carole joined her in the tack room.

"You really think so?" Carole asked anxiously.

"Yes. He seemed more under control."

Carole smiled. "Spoken like a true friend, Lisa."

"No, I mean it. He was wilder yesterday."

Carole sat down beside Lisa and picked up a pair of reins to oil. In one sense, Lisa was right. Samson had been calmer today. But Carole thought that that was just a fluke. Maybe he had run around more in the pasture and had less energy. The fact was the colt wasn't

24

responding to their training. Every time they put the saddle on him, he acted as if the whole thing was a big game. A couple of times he had practically run right over whoever was leading him.

"What do you think our next step should be?" Carole asked.

"I was thinking about that. Obviously we can't go on the way we have been . . . unless we want him to learn some very bad habits." Lisa paused to see how Carole would react to what she was saying.

"I agree," Carole said, her face serious.

"Okay, then," Lisa continued, "we have to do what we always do when something isn't working: change tactics. I thought maybe we could put one stirrup on the saddle, and someone could walk alongside him holding the stirrup in place so it wouldn't bang against his side. Then slowly we could stop holding it and see what he does."

"Okay, and then next week when Stevie's back, we could try both stirrups," Carole said.

As they worked oil into sets of reins, nosebands, and cheek straps, the girls brainstormed on other ways to get past Samson's problem with the stirrups. Both of them were optimistic that something would work soon. "But even if it takes a while, it doesn't matter. We have as much time as we need. We could even put the stirrups aside for a few weeks and see if Samson forgets about not liking them," Lisa pointed out.

Carole nodded. "I keep forgetting that, but you're right. We don't need to rush him at all."

The tack room door swung open and Max stepped inside. "I thought I heard voices, and I'm glad to see that the voices belong to tack cleaners," Max said approvingly. "But wait . . . where's the third musketeer?"

Like everyone else at Pine Hollow, Max was so accustomed to seeing The Saddle Club together that he always noticed when one of the girls was missing.

"She's visiting relatives in New Jersey," Carole explained.

"I see. So the two of you are doing the work of three, hmm?" Max inquired.

"Naturally," said Lisa, without missing a beat. "We both rode, we took Belle out for a walk, we worked with Samson, and now we're oiling one and a half times our normal number of bridles."

Max grinned. "Just what I wanted to hear. I'm taking a few of the adult students to a dressage show this weekend, and I'm not sure they understand the meaning of the word 'preparation.' I haven't seen any of them cleaning tack yet."

The girls laughed. They were glad to help Max out in a pinch.

"Oh, and I'm glad you mentioned Samson," Max continued. "I've been meaning to tell you that I've decided to send him to Mr. Grover's to finish his training. Since I don't have the time to train him myself, I think he'll do nicely there."

Carole and Lisa both stopped polishing in midstroke. They looked at each other as if to make sure they had heard right. Unaware of the bombshell he had just dropped, Max began checking over the tack he needed for the weekend, whistling as he worked.

Carole cleared her throat nervously. "So, is this decision definite?" she asked.

"Why, yes, it is," Max replied. He gave Carole and Lisa a sharp look. "Why the long faces? Scott Grover's an excellent trainer—one of the best."

"I know, but—" Carole began, but stopped herself. She knew better than to argue with Max, but she was shocked that he would take the colt from his home and from the people who knew and loved him and put him in an unfamiliar barn to be trained by a total stranger.

"So it doesn't matter that Mr. Grover doesn't know Samson?" Lisa asked. Carole was glad to find that Lisa's thoughts mirrored her own.

27

"Not really, no. That's what it means to be a professional: You can train any horse. Of course, in an ideal world, the trainer would know the horse from the very beginning—say, from birth even, but it's not necessary."

Lisa and Carole exchanged glances again. They *had* known Samson from birth. Didn't that count for anything?

"We sure have watched Samson grow up," Carole said pointedly, hoping Max would get the hint.

"Yeah, I'll never forget the day he was born," Lisa chimed in. "We were all there."

"It was an exciting day. You girls were with him from the beginning," Max agreed. He paused and his eyes rested on Lisa and Carole. "You know how much I appreciate all the work you've done with the colt, don't you?"

"Ye-es," Carole said tentatively. She wasn't sure what Max was getting at. If he appreciated it so much, why wasn't he going to let them continue? Did he know about the problems they'd been having lately?

"Good," Max said briskly. "Because you've been a great help—all three of you."

Finally Carole couldn't hold her tongue any longer. "But then—"

"Look," Max cut her off. "I think I know what's coming, but you have to understand that there comes a time when a horse needs to be professionally trained. Samson has reached the point where he needs the hand of an expert guiding him. Think about it: That stirrup problem isn't just going to go away on its own. Okay?" With that, Max turned on his heel and left the room.

Carole stared after him in shock. So Max had known! But then why hadn't he said something instead of springing this on them?

"He obviously doesn't think we're up to the job," Carole said grimly, when Max was safely out of earshot. "So he's decided to take Samson away."

"Gosh, I guess you're right," Lisa conceded. It seemed odd that Max had reacted so fast to their difficulties without informing them of his plan.

"So much for forgetting about the stirrups for a few weeks. We've got to straighten things out this weekend or else," Carole said.

"You mean you think if we get Samson to tolerate the stirrups Max will let him stay?" Lisa asked.

"Definitely. I'm sure that's why he suddenly decided to send him to a trainer—he thinks we can't solve this problem." Carole stood to hang up the bridle she'd been oiling. "Luckily, Max is going to be at that dressage show, so we'll have plenty of time."

29

Lisa nodded thoughtfully. "I guess it can't hurt."

"Can't hurt? It's our only chance to keep Samson here," Carole replied.

"Okay, then," Lisa said after a minute, "count me in."

"LILA, YOU'VE OUTDONE yourself," Stevie's father remarked, putting his fork down. The two families had just finished a huge steak dinner. "If the caterer on Sunday is half as good, there won't be a bite left."

"I hope you still have room for dessert—it's éclairs," Stevie's aunt replied.

Stevie licked her lips in anticipation. "I for one can definitely squeeze in a few bites of an éclair," she said, grinning.

"Not me, Mom. No matter what dress I wear Sunday, I have to be able to fit into it," Angie said. "And besides, I'm saving myself for the chocolate mousse and the hazelnut torte we're having then."

Suddenly Stevie didn't feel quite so hungry. If Angie was turning into one of those thin girls who always acted like she had to go on a diet, Stevie didn't want to hear about it.

"Two desserts, huh?" Alex asked, sounding impressed.

"Three if you count the birthday cake," Angie replied.

"Hey, remember that time we made a carrot cake, but nobody would eat it so we tried feeding it to the horses?"

30

Stevie asked suddenly. The memory made her laugh. Even Sparkles and the hunters had refused the girls' concoction.

"I'm not sure," Angie replied vaguely.

"Really?" Stevie said, surprised. "Boy, I remember it like it was yesterday. Sparkles looked so funny when he turned his nose up at it. Then again, he always was a fussy eater, wasn't he? My horse, Belle, can be picky, too. Sometimes—"

"Do tell us, Stevie. We're all dying to know exactly what Belle eats for breakfast, lunch, and dinner," Chad commented.

"That's right," Alex piped up. "Please continue. And don't let anyone tell you that you have a one-track mind and you only talk about horses. We *know* it isn't true."

Stevie clamped her mouth shut and fixed her brothers with the evil eye. Naturally, they would tease *her* about being single-minded. And yet they didn't seem to notice that all anyone *else* had talked about was the sweet sixteen party. Between their arrival and dinner, Stevie had learned: the reasons Angie's party was going to be better than anyone else's; the gifts Angie was expecting to get (none of them was even remotely horse-related); and the Latin names of the flowers Angie and her mother had ordered. Honestly, Stevie would have thought her

31

brothers would be glad to have the subject changed to horses.

"Did you know that there are different colors of caviar?" Angie was saying. "There's black, red . . ."

Stevie sighed. The long weekend was beginning to look very long indeed.

On Saturday morning Carole and Lisa arrived at Pine Hollow bright and early. They were planning to spend the whole day with Samson. They wouldn't train him for more than half an hour at a time, but they wanted to be around him as much as possible. That way, there would be absolutely nothing special about their presence—nothing that would alarm him or give him an excuse to act up.

"The coast is clear," Lisa announced, rejoining Carole by the colt's stall. She had checked the parking lot to make sure the Pine Hollow van was gone. It wasn't that

33

they thought Max would mind their working with Samson some more, but they did feel a little sheepish after what he'd said the day before about the "stirrup problem." Besides, if they could fix the problem by the time the weekend was over, it would be a perfect surprise.

"Good, because Samson seems calm and quiet," Carole responded.

"You know, I think we may just get him to snap out of it today," Lisa said optimistically. "It's not like this is a huge problem. And Samson is an intelligent horse."

"He *is* intelligent," Carole agreed. "Right, boy?" She gave his withers a scratch. Once they had decided to devote the whole weekend to Samson, Carole felt much more relaxed. She'd stayed up half the night reading training books and jotting down practical ideas that seemed related to Samson's behavior. Plus she had one idea that wasn't so practical, which she shared with Lisa. "We shouldn't need it, but let's touch the horseshoe anyway, for a little extra luck."

The good-luck horseshoe was a Pine Hollow tradition. Normally students touched it before mounting, but Carole figured it could work for training, too.

"Good idea. After all," Lisa pointed out, "you can never have too much luck."

*   *   *

34

"WHOA, I FORGOT how big Birdie is," Stevie remarked. She was sitting atop the Lakes' sixteen-point-three-hand Thoroughbred-Clydesdale cross, as she and Angie headed out for a midmorning ride. Stevie had always liked the contrast between "Birdie," the petite, feminine-sounding name, and Birdie, the half-draft horse gelding. "He's a fun change from my horse," Stevie added.

Angie didn't seem to hear.

It had taken Stevie a while to convince Angie to go riding at all. Finally Aunt Lila had told Angie that she was driving her crazy asking about party details and had better get out of the house for a couple of hours. "Belle's only fifteen-point-one," Stevie went on. She hoped Angie would pick up on her comment and ask her to describe Belle, but her cousin just smiled vaguely and clucked to Sparkles to keep walking.

"I also forgot how much colder February would be in New Jersey," Stevie said, persisting. "At Pine Hollow the ground hardly ever freezes like this." She paused to see if Angie would react at all.

After a minute, Angie seemed to realize that she should say something to be polite. "What was that? Pine Hollow?" she asked.

"Right. That's the place I told you about, where we

ride. I keep Belle there, and my two best friends ride there, too. You should see it. It's got a big indoor ring and—"

"Speaking of friends, did I tell you who was going to be at the party?" Angie asked, slowing Sparkles so that Stevie could ride next to her on Birdie.

"Yes, you did," Stevie lied. She knew she sounded annoyed, but she couldn't help it. The subject of the party was beginning to make her feel nauseated. "But you never told me why you didn't take Sparkles to a lot of shows last season."

"Look, I just like riding him for fun now, okay?" Angie said defensively.

"Yeah, sure—definitely," Stevie said, biting her tongue so she wouldn't say anything else. The way her cousin sounded, she knew better than to press the subject any further. But it did seem too bad that a talented jumper like Sparkles would never again meet the challenge of showing. Pleasure riding was great, but it didn't seem enough for Sparkles. Not knowing what else to say, Stevie gave up. It seemed like the best thing to do would be to settle back, enjoy the ride, and resign herself to listening to Angie describe the guest list, as she had just begun to do.

"Let's just say it's all the coolest kids from school. The guys in Voyager—"

"What's Voyager?"

"That's the name of the band!" Angie half-cried. "Gosh, Stevie, you're getting forgetful. Anyway, there are four of them, and they're all *juniors*. You should see Ted Capuano—he's one of the best hockey players in the school, not to mention one of the best-looking. He plays bass. And then there's Jeff on drums and Kevin and Mike on guitars—Mike is Val's boyfriend. Of course Val is coming too because she's on the cheerleading squad and *they're* all coming—"

Stevie couldn't help rolling her eyes. "Why would you invite the cheerleading squad?" she asked. She remembered a discussion she'd once had with Angie about how lame they thought it was to cheer for other teams when you could play something yourself—or better yet, ride.

Angie gave Stevie an odd look. "We spend a lot of time together, what with practice every afternoon and the games. The other cheerleaders are my best friends. Naturally, I'd want to invite them to my party."

Stevie did a double take. It was one thing for her fun, down-to-earth cousin to start dressing up and wearing makeup. But now she was a cheerleader? Stevie could hardly believe it. She stared wordlessly at Angie as the older girl began to name all the football players who might show up. *Football players?* Stevie thought. *What on earth has gotten into Angie?*

Suddenly Stevie had a sneaking suspicion. There was a phrase that adults used all the time about girls who rode. Stevie hated it, and if anyone ever said it to her, she got so angry she wanted to clobber them. It was: "She may like horses now, but wait until she discovers boys." Stevie, Carole, and Lisa all agreed that it was a completely dumb thing to say. They had all "discovered" boys, and it hadn't made them like horses one bit less. In fact, one of the reasons Stevie liked her boyfriend, Phil Marsten, so much was that he was as crazy about horses as she was. Carole had felt the same way about her almost-boyfriend Cam. Before Cam moved, he and Carole had shared some wonderful times together—many of them around horses. And the same went for Lisa and any boy she'd ever liked.

And yet the awful saying seemed to apply to Angie. Now that she had cool friends at school and knew the football players and the guys in a band, she didn't seem to care the slightest bit about riding. The way she was sitting on Sparkles summed up her whole attitude toward horses. She was slouching in the saddle, letting Sparkles dog along on a loose rein. She still had a basically good position—heels down, hands light on the reins—but it was obvious that she didn't care how she looked. At least, not on a horse. Her dress for the party was another story.

38

Party, party, party! The more Stevie heard about the party, the more boring it sounded. Angie didn't even have any fun games or activities planned; apparently everyone was going to stand around and eat and listen to the band the whole time. Even that could be tolerable if the people were nice, but Stevie was betting that her cousin's friends would be as boring as Angie seemed to have become. They probably wouldn't know how to have fun. They sounded like the kind of friends that Veronica diAngelo would have. As for the other relatives who would be coming, Angie had barely mentioned them.

At least Chad, Alex, and Michael will be there, Stevie thought. Then she laughed out loud. Lisa and Carole would never let her forget it if she told them that she was *glad* that her brothers would be at a party because she wanted to hang out with them more than anyone else.

Beside her, Angie picked up a trot, motioning for Stevie to follow. "I can finish telling you later," Angie called.

"Great," Stevie muttered, wondering if her cousin would catch the sarcasm that she was finding hard to keep out of her voice. Wistfully she thought of Lisa and Carole back at Pine Hollow, training Samson. If only she could be there, too. Even the stirrup problem

39

couldn't be harder than putting up with Angie and her never-ending party talk for three days.

SHAKING HER HEAD despondently, Lisa reached up and unbuckled Samson's girth. Once again, she and Carole were taking the saddle off the colt, hoping he would relax and forget about the stirrups. It was the second time that morning that they'd saddled him up only to untack him ten minutes later. They had tried putting only one stirrup on the saddle and having Lisa, then Carole, hold it in place while Samson walked. But the strange positioning of the person helping seemed to excite him even more. The worst part was that they always started out trying to encourage the colt but ended up trying to discipline him. Then they were back at square one, but with a sweaty horse who needed to be cooled off. All of the optimism of the morning had faded.

It was rare for two members of The Saddle Club to be too dejected to talk to one another, but as the girls walked Samson, each of them was lost in her own thoughts about what they should do.

After a lap or two around the ring, a familiar face appeared at the door. "Hi, girls, how's it going?" Mrs. Reg inquired.

Lisa and Carole exchanged glances. Mrs. Reg was

Max's mother, so anything they said would probably get straight back to Max. Reluctantly they led Samson over to the older woman.

Trying to sound normal, Carole spoke up. "He's not perfect yet, but he's getting there," she said.

"A little more work and he'll be just fine," Lisa said to back her up.

Mrs. Reg smiled benevolently. "Good, I'm glad to hear it. You know, I was thinking about something today, and I wanted to tell you girls."

This time, instead of looking at one another, Lisa elbowed Carole. Mrs. Reg was famous around the stables for her long, drawn-out, confusing stories. Whenever she told one, she got a faraway look in her eye—like the one she had right now. Sure enough, she launched in.

"When my husband Max was young—you know, Max's father, Max the Second—he wanted to be an architect. As much as he loved horses and riding, he didn't think running a stable would be a very exciting career. His father, the one you call Max the First, wanted him to take over Pine Hollow one day—naturally—and they had plenty of arguments about it. But finally Max the First agreed to send his son to college to study architecture." With that, Mrs. Reg stopped to give Samson a pat. "All right, girls, I'll catch up with you later."

"Wait!" Lisa and Carole wailed in unison. Mrs. Reg looked surprised.

"You haven't finished telling us the story," Carole said.

"Oh, I suppose you're right. But there isn't really any more to tell," replied Mrs. Reg.

"But what happened? Did Max the Second become an architect?" Lisa asked.

"An architect?" said Mrs. Reg. "Oh, no. After a couple of years he changed his major to accounting."

"Really? Why?" Carole inquired.

"Well, he decided that he *did* want to return to run Pine Hollow with his father after all. He thought a business background would be useful to help him keep the books."

"But what happened to make him change his mind?" Lisa asked, exasperated. It was typical of Mrs. Reg to tell a story and never get to the point of it.

"Well, part of it was that architecture wasn't quite as exciting as he'd imagined. But the main thing was that he had taken a part-time job at a stable near the university to help with expenses. The stable manager there became a mentor to him and he helped inspire Max's decision."

After Mrs. Reg finished, she wished the girls luck with

their training, gave Samson a final pat, and headed out of the ring. Lisa and Carole stood in silence for a minute once she was gone.

"Do you have any idea . . . ?" Carole asked finally, not bothering to finish the question.

"What on earth she was getting at?" Lisa ventured.

"Exactly."

"Absolutely none."

"Me either," Carole said with a shrug.

The girls always liked hearing Regnery family history—it certainly was interesting—but they were stumped about why Mrs. Reg was telling it now. In any case, they didn't have much time to think about it. They had to get back to work with Samson.

"Any ideas?" Carole asked, turning to Lisa.

Lisa put her hands on her hips determinedly. "We've just got to think of something. . . . I know: Let's pretend Stevie's here. Without her, we're one brain short. But we can at least try to think of what she would do."

Carole liked the idea. She and Lisa decided to walk Samson a little more and then have a pretend "Stevie brainstorm" after putting the colt away. They could eat lunch at the same time and then resume training in the afternoon.

"One thing's for sure: Stevie's having a better time than we are this weekend," Lisa said.

Carole nodded. "You can say that again. Riding with her horsey cousin, going to a great party—sounds like a dream weekend, doesn't it?"

THE RIDE TOOK up part of the morning, but as soon as lunch was over Stevie was bored out of her mind again. When her father suggested that the family go into Philadelphia for some afternoon sightseeing and dinner, Stevie was thrilled.

"We'll get out of the way for a few hours and give Angie and Lila some time to take care of a few party preparations by themselves," Mr. Lake said, as he and Stevie hunted through the bookshelves for a Philadelphia guidebook.

"You don't have to explain to me, Dad," Stevie replied. "I can't wait to get out of the house and stay out. If I hear the word 'canapé' one more time today, I'll scream." Her father's raised eyebrows told her that she had gone quite far enough.

There was no guidebook to be found, but Chad said that with his knowledge of American history they wouldn't need one anyway.

"And to think I'd convinced myself that I wanted to spend some time with my brothers," Stevie muttered to herself, following the boys out to the driveway.

In a matter of minutes, Uncle Chester, who had decided to join them, and the six Willow Creek Lakes were seated in the van and buzzing toward Philadelphia.

"It's the city of brotherly love and the original capital of this country," Chad announced. "Probably not something you'd know much about, Stevie," he added.

"Brotherly love? Yeah, that would be a change," Stevie shot back with a triumphant grin.

"Almost as big a change as your deciding to become an actual girl like Angie," Alex said, doubling over with laughter at his own joke.

"Imagine if Stevie joined the cheerleading squad!" Michael remarked.

Chad put up a hand. "Please, Michael: Even *my* imagination has its limits!"

"I wonder if it'll ever happen," Alex mused aloud.

"What?" asked Michael.

"That Stevie will turn into the sister we've never had," said Alex.

Chad frowned, pretending to concentrate. "I just can't see it. What I *can* see is Stevie attending her senior prom in jeans and riding boots."

"You know what I can see?" Stevie asked. Without waiting for an answer, she continued, "Three boys. All of them trying to impress a bunch of cheerleaders at a certain birthday party, when all of a sudden, somebody starts to tell embarrassing secrets about them in a really loud voice . . ."

THE FIRST STOP in Philadelphia was Independence Hall and the Liberty Bell. Stevie's brothers had either been convinced by her threat in the car or were distracted by the sights. In any case, they stopped teasing long enough to act like tourists.

"Do you know why it's called Independence Hall?" Chad asked, when the group had assembled outside the building. "Because this is where the U.S. proclaimed itself free from England, in the Declaration of Independence. I just finished a school project on the American Revolution."

"Do you know what year the Declaration was, Chad?" Uncle Chester asked as they all started up the stairs.

47

"That's easy. 1776," Chad replied.

"Correct you are. Say, since you've just finished studying it, how about you tell us some more about that period, in honor of Presidents' Day," Uncle Chester suggested.

"Good idea, Chester. Chad can be our tour guide," Mr. Lake agreed.

Stevie grimaced as Chad drew himself up proudly. Somehow she knew she was in for a long, boring lecture that would show off Chad's knowledge of colonial history.

"Sure," Chad said eagerly. "Let's see . . . well, the Declaration was written by Thomas Jefferson. And John Hancock was the first to sign it—his signature is the biggest and showiest. The colonists thought that everyone was entitled to 'Life, Liberty, and the Pursuit of Happiness,' or, at least, that's how Jefferson put it. When they proclaimed the Declaration, they rang the Liberty Bell, which we're about to see."

In a few minutes the Lake group had surrounded the famous bell. "The bell was hidden during the British occupation of Philadelphia," Chad explained. "You can see it's been cracked twice, but that happened later, in the nineteenth century."

Beside him, Stevie was seething with jealousy. She almost wished her brothers would start teasing her again.

At least then she wouldn't have to put up with Chad's giving a history lesson. Her parents and Uncle Chester looked so impressed it made Stevie feel ill. After all, anyone could learn a little history. What was the big deal?

"The King of England at the time—"

"Yes, yes, we know, Chad," Stevie heard herself say, surprised that her mouth had opened by itself.

"No, no—go on, I'm interested," Uncle Chester protested.

"We're *all* interested," said Stevie's mother, with a warning look at Stevie.

Stevie couldn't help it. Her ultracompetitive spirit had kicked in. She was sure she could play tour guide as well as Chad.

"The King of England was—" Chad began again.

"George the Second," Stevie jumped in. She waited for everyone to look as pleased with her information as they seemed to be with Chad's.

"I don't think so," said Mrs. Lake.

"Good try, Stevie," Chad said, grinning. "But you mean George the Third."

"Second? Third? What's the difference?" Stevie said, in a feeble attempt at a joke. "In any case, everyone drank tea in Boston to celebrate the Revolution."

The whole family looked at her blankly. "Actually,

49

Stevie, the Boston Tea Party wasn't a party at all. The colonists didn't drink the tea: They dumped it—into Boston Harbor, to protest George the Third's high taxes," Chad informed her.

"You sure know your history, Chad," Uncle Chester commented. "I think that's great."

"Excuse me, I need some air," Stevie gasped. She pushed by the group and into the next room and collapsed on the nearest bench. Behind her, she could hear Chad droning on. A few words floated out to her: "Concord," "Lexington." Then, all of a sudden, she heard, "Paul Revere."

"Aha!" Stevie said, jumping up. She tore past a few bewildered tourists and back into the room. "On April 18, 1775, Paul Revere, a well-known silversmith, rode from Boston to Lexington to warn Massachusetts that the British were coming. His ride was immortalized in a poem written by Henry Wadsworth Longfellow which begins, 'Listen, my children, and you shall hear/Of the midnight ride of Paul Revere.' How do you like that, Chad, huh? Pretty good, eh? Gotcha! Gotcha!"

Mrs. Lake put a hand on Stevie's forehead. "Do you feel all right, dear? Did you catch cold out on that ride this morning?" she asked.

"Mom, I feel fine! And I'm right, aren't I, Chad?" Stevie demanded.

"Yes, you are right," said Chad, eyeing her suspiciously. "I was just getting to that part. Let's see . . ."

"Oh, I get it!" Alex exclaimed suddenly. "It's Paul Revere's *ride*. It's part of history with a *horse* in it. That's why Stevie remembered it!"

Everyone sighed with relief. "That explains it," Chad responded. "Now, where was I?"

Stevie opened her mouth to protest but then stopped. The truth was the only other fact she could seem to remember from her U.S. history unit was the name of Ulysses S. Grant's horse. It was Traveler. Resolving to have Lisa brush her up on the rest of the stuff, she trailed grumpily after the group.

AFTER INDEPENDENCE HALL, the Lakes wandered around Society Hill for a couple of hours and then went downtown to Center City. Since Mr. and Mrs. Lake were busy lawyers in Washington, D.C., they didn't have much time for shopping. They were looking forward to the prospect of some leisurely browsing. They also planned to get a birthday present for Angie.

"Sorry, Stevie, no tack shop here," Alex announced as they entered Wannamaker's, a department store on one end of the shopping mall. "You'll have to go to normal stores with the rest of us."

"But there is a bookstore—in case you want to buy a

textbook on American history," Chad joked. He, Alex, and Michael cracked up.

"That's funny," Stevie responded, "I was going to suggest that you head for the bookstore, Chad, and pick up a few *self-help* books. There should be one on learning not to show off. And then the three of you could get an etiquette book—after all, it's never too late to try to learn good manners."

Mrs. Lake spun around, her hands on her hips. "All right, enough—all of you. I'm getting pretty tired of your bickering. We'll split up and meet back here in an hour and a half. And I don't expect to hear any arguing after that. Got it?"

"I can hardly wait," Stevie said.

"Me either," Chad agreed.

The minute their parents and Uncle Chester had departed, Chad turned to Stevie. "So, what do you want to do?"

Stevie shrugged. "I don't know—you?"

It never failed: As soon as they were told to split up or were sent to their rooms as punishment for fighting, Stevie and her brothers would immediately make up and hang out together.

"Can we go to the toy store? I want to look at the G.I. Joes," said Michael.

"Sounds good to me," said Alex, as the four of them trooped off together.

THE GROUP REGATHERED at the appointed time by the huge eagle statue near the Wannamaker's entrance. Mr. and Mrs. Lake had bought Angie a bath oil-perfume set, and Mrs. Lake had gotten herself a new lipstick for the party. Stevie, Chad, and Alex had hung out in the toy store with Michael, and they'd all chipped in for a deck of cards to use on the train ride home Monday. Since it was too cold to wander around anymore and everybody was hungry, the seven of them went back to the van and then drove to Bookbinders, a famous old Philadelphia seafood restaurant.

The food at Bookbinders was delicious—or so Stevie gathered. By the time her stuffed shrimp arrived, she could barely eat them. She felt stuffed herself after polishing off most of the rolls in the bread basket and gulping down two Shirley Temples waiting for dinner. Still, she insisted on ordering dessert and managed to cram in a few bites of mud pie. That was the problem with nice restaurants, Stevie decided. There was so much good food you couldn't appreciate it all.

After dinner, Uncle Chester drove the van across town so they could see the Philadelphia Art Museum and Boathouse Row by night. The river that cut through that part of the city was called the Schuylkill, pronounced "*Skool*-kill," according to Chad. Along the dark strip of water, the small buildings where the city's rowing clubs stored their shells and oars were draped with twinkling white lights that were mirrored by the river. It was a beautiful sight—especially when a gentle snow began to fall. Soon the few flakes turned to a picturesque flurry. In Virginia it hardly ever snowed; when it did, the snow was usually patchy and didn't stick, so this northern flurry was a treat. Watching the ground whiten, Stevie could even forgive Chad for announcing that "Schuylkill" meant "hidden river" in Dutch.

As they sped along, Stevie pressed her face against the van window and peered out at the city lights. If only Carole and Lisa had been there to enjoy the sights with her . . . they could have had so much fun traipsing around together. Even when they weren't around horses, the girls seemed to get into adventures. All things considered, Stevie did have to admit that Chad, Alex, and Michael hadn't been that bad. But she dreaded the next day, when she would have to deal with them around a bunch of cheerleaders. That was when Stevie would *really* miss her friends. She wasn't entirely sure that she could survive the sweet sixteen party-of-the-century without them.

6

"KNOCK, KNOCK! Pizza delivery!" a voice called from outside.

"Pizza delivery? When did you call to order?" Lisa asked Carole. After Pine Hollow, the two girls had adjourned to Carole's house, where Lisa was spending the night.

Carole grinned. "I didn't, but when Dad has to work late, he makes up for it by getting pizza. Or if he's really late, it's Chinese takeout," she explained. She went to let her father in. "Is this the Hanson special I asked for?" she inquired through the door.

Joining Carole at the door, Lisa raised her eyebrows in curiosity. She and Stevie had spent many a night at the Hansons' and they were used to the special rapport between Carole and her father, but Lisa had never heard of the "Hanson special."

"As long as the Hanson special is still a large, half plain, half mushroom-and-pepperoni," Colonel Hanson replied, chuckling.

Carole swung open the door. "Excellent memory, sir. You may come in."

With a kiss for his daughter and a warm hello for Lisa, Colonel Hanson handed the pizza to them. Then he went to wash up in the bathroom while the girls set the table. Soon the three of them were seated around the kitchen table, attacking the hot slices.

"I apologize for being so late," Colonel Hanson said between bites. As a high-ranking officer in the Marines, Carole's father was responsible for a number of projects at the nearby Quantico military base. One of his main duties was supervising the hundreds of men below him.

"What happened, Dad?" Carole asked. "You don't usually get stuck on the weekends."

"No, I don't. I can't tell you the details because it's classified, but, basically, an eager young officer bit off more than he could chew. He took on a big project that was above his head, and he ended up causing more problems than he solved. He wanted to help, but he just didn't have the experience. That's why I was so late: I spent the whole day fixing somebody else's mistakes."

"That's got to be frustrating," said Lisa.

"It sure is," Colonel Hanson agreed. For a moment he was quiet, lost in thought.

To take his mind off his long day, Carole and Lisa began to tell him about theirs. Colonel Hanson knew all about Samson, although Carole hadn't gotten a chance to tell him about the stirrup problem. She summed it up briefly.

"Hmm . . . so he's not getting any better at all?" Colonel Hanson asked when Carole had finished.

Knowing it was still a touchy subject, Lisa decided to let Carole answer the question. "Not yet," Carole replied. The two girls' attempt at Stevie-like brainstorming had completely failed. All they had been able to think of were jokes that Stevie might have told, and even those hadn't been up to her caliber.

"You think so, too, Lisa?" Colonel Hanson inquired.

Lisa nodded. "It's becoming a habit, his misbehaving when we put the saddle on. He seems to think it's his designated playtime. And the whole point of training him with natural horsemanship is that the horse and the trainer are supposed to work together, not be on opposite sides. But when he starts acting up and fooling around, we can't just ignore it."

"That certainly sounds true," Colonel Hanson agreed. "You know, I can't offer much practical advice, but I do empathize with you. It seems like you're stuck for the time being. Maybe it would be better to forget the stirrups and move on to something else."

"But that's just it, Dad: We can't," said Carole. She explained Max's plan to send Samson away for further training, unless they could conquer the problem right away.

Expecting her father to be sympathetic, Carole was surprised when, after a thoughtful pause, he responded, "I hate to say this, honey, because I know how attached you girls are to that colt, but maybe Max's idea isn't such a bad one. Sometimes you need to call in reinforcements to get the job done."

After a minute, Lisa hesitantly agreed. "I—I think so, too," she said.

Carole shot her friend a shocked look. She couldn't believe Lisa was ready to give up! She'd thought the whole Saddle Club was committed to training Samson. Period. "How can you both say that? I mean—" Abruptly, Carole stopped. She could feel her face getting flushed and knew she was in danger of losing her temper in front of Lisa. The very thought of Samson's leaving made her miserable. She looked down at the slice of pizza on her plate, suddenly feeling sick to her stomach. "It just seems wrong at this point, after we've worked so hard getting him to trust us," she said. Everyone was quiet for a minute.

Colonel Hanson cut short the awkward pause by changing the subject and asking about Stevie's trip. For the rest of the meal, they all talked about other things. It wasn't until after dinner, when the girls were getting ready for bed, that Carole asked Lisa to explain her change of heart.

"It's simple," Lisa said, choosing her words carefully. "I think Max and your father may be right—maybe Samson does need someone more experienced than The Saddle Club to help him through the next stages of his training. It's not as if any of us has actually trained a young horse all the way. If we mess up now we could ruin Samson for his career as a pleasure horse. It's like what happened to your father, only somebody would have to spend years undoing our mistakes instead of one day."

"But our situation is completely different," Carole said, her voice urgent. "We're not like that Marine because we *do* know what we're doing. Maybe we haven't trained hundreds of horses, but do you honestly think we're going to ruin Samson?"

59

"Right now, no," Lisa admitted. "He's just having a good time being silly with us. But we're not exactly getting anywhere with him, either," she added gently.

"If only we had more time," Carole said.

"But how much time would we need? Carole, you've said in the past that training doesn't go by a timetable. You can never tell how long you'll have to work with a particular horse to teach him a particular skill."

Carole shrugged, her jaw set.

Lisa argued a little more, but then let the matter drop. The truth was Lisa privately thought that Samson might even have regressed in his training. Today he had been finicky about the way they put the bridle on, as if he seemed to know that he could play without anything happening to him. But she couldn't just come right out and tell Carole. She knew that Carole feared "losing" Samson because of the way she had lost Cobalt. That was why Carole couldn't be objective and rational about this situation. Lisa herself wasn't eager to see the colt leave Pine Hollow, even temporarily. But Colonel Hanson was right: They were stuck.

"Hey, I've got an idea. Let's call Stevie," Lisa suggested, hoping to clear the air. "That way we won't have to imagine what she's thinking."

Carole brightened visibly. "Okay. You have the number she gave you, right?"

Lisa had written the New Jersey Lakes' phone number in her address book. She pulled the book out of her overnight bag, dialed, and held the receiver between her and Carole's ears.

STEVIE WAS SITTING in the window seat of her cousin's living room, staring out the window at the snow drifting down. She was trying to think of a way she could escape from the room so that she wouldn't have to listen to the never-ending party discussion going on around her when the phone rang.

Let's see, she mused. *Is it the caterer again? Or maybe the florist? Or could it be one of the ten million zillion invited guests?* She cocked an ear to hear what her aunt was saying and to her surprise heard her own name called.

"Stevie! It's two friends of yours on the telephone. Why don't you take it in here?" Aunt Lila suggested.

Stevie didn't need to be told twice. She raced for the kitchen and lunged for the receiver. It was Carole and Lisa! "Gosh, I feel like I haven't spoken to you guys in two *years*!" Stevie said. "What's up? Tell me everything."

Carole and Lisa didn't waste words since it was a long-distance call. They immediately filled Stevie in on the Samson situation.

"You're kidding!" Stevie exclaimed, horrified, when

61

they had finished their breathless account. "Max is really going to send Samson away?" She agreed wholeheartedly with The Saddle Club's counterplan to prove to Max that Pine Hollow was the best place for the colt's training.

Stevie had realized there were some problems, but it wasn't as if they were serious. And if Lisa's and Carole's one extra day at Pine Hollow hadn't helped, a few more certainly would. "There's no way he should go to Mr. Grover's! We're the ones who know him and love him," Stevie said firmly.

On the other end of the phone, Lisa found herself getting caught up in Stevie's enthusiasm. The way Stevie put it, letting a professional take over was an easy way out that Max would naturally want to take. But it didn't take into consideration the fact that The Saddle Club was more dedicated and sensitive than a professional who had several horses to train at a time. Carole didn't need to be convinced.

"I just wish I could be there to help," Stevie said. She felt helpless being stuck in New Jersey.

"We know you're here in spirit," Carole said, "so just enjoy the party, and we'll see you when you get back."

"Enjoy?" Stevie repeated, incredulous. "Oh my gosh, I forgot you guys don't know."

"Know what?" Lisa demanded.

Stevie lowered her voice to a murmur so that she wouldn't be overheard. "Only that my horsey cousin is now a boy-crazy cheerleader!"

"She is?" Carole said, grimacing at Lisa.

"Yup. And she sounds as if she could be Veronica diAngelo's best friend. She's spent the last twenty-four hours discussing herself, her friends on the football team, and what she's going to wear. Oh, and the food. I can't take it anymore! And the worst thing is my three brothers act like they're interested in the whole thing!"

"What about riding? Have you at least gotten out on the horses?" Lisa asked.

"For about twenty minutes," Stevie replied scornfully. "Then Angie decided it was too cold for her. She didn't want the air to dry out her complexion!"

Carole and Lisa groaned in unison. "Gosh, here we've been envisioning the perfect weekend in New Jersey," Lisa said.

"It is perfect," Stevie said kiddingly, "perfect for Angie, the cheerleaders, the football team . . ."

The girls talked until the doorbell at the Lakes' rang and Stevie said, reluctantly, that she'd better hang up.

As she put the phone down, loud shouts of greeting came from the hallway. Stevie peeked her head out to see who had arrived. It was more relatives—Angie's aunt and uncle on her mother's side, the Davisons, and their two little girls, Ginny and Beth. After introductions all around, Aunt Lila got everyone settled in the living room with coffee or hot chocolate.

"Phew! It's a relief to be here," said Bob Davison, relaxing in an easy chair. "For a while, we weren't sure if we were going to make it with the snow."

"So the weathermen were right? It's really turning into a big storm?" Aunt Lila asked anxiously.

"I'll say. New England already has about eight inches, and it's supposed to snow all night," said Lila's sister, Peg. "It's what you call a nor'easter—the storm is moving southwest. We'll probably get the brunt of it within a day."

"How are the roads?" Stevie inquired from her perch on the window seat.

At her question, the grownups turned. Stevie didn't mind that they looked surprised at her jumping into the adult conversation. Even discussion about the weather was a welcome change—Stevie was ready to talk about absolutely any subject other than the sweet sixteen party. She could have listened to a speech about the three-toed sloth for all she cared.

"They aren't too bad, at least not down here. In Connecticut the backroads were starting to get icy, but once we reached the highway, we were fine," Peg answered.

Stevie saw her aunt and uncle exchange worried looks. "If the storm continues . . ." Uncle Chester didn't finish his sentence. Instead he got up to look out the window where Stevie was sitting.

"What does it look like?" Angie demanded. All at once, she seemed to have realized the importance of the weather.

"It's fine," said Uncle Chester, relief in his voice. "It's still coming down gently."

"Good," said Angie. Then she crossed her arms over her chest defiantly. "Not that I'm worried or anything. After all this planning, Mother Nature wouldn't dare storm on the day of the party!" she declared.

SUNDAY MORNING DAWNED cold and gray in New Jersey. Stevie turned over and pulled her down comforter tighter around her. It was half past ten, but she was hoping to stay in bed as late as possible to avoid the final party preparations. With one hand, she reached out and lifted the window shade to check the weather. There were a few inches of snow on the ground from the night before, but the plow had already been by and cleared the roads. A few snowflakes drifted down out of the uniformly gray sky. Only time would tell whether the storm was going to hit full force.

66

Resting her head back on the pillow, Stevie thought of how much fun it would be to take a ride in the new snow. All of the horses' shoes had been pulled for the winter, so there was no danger of snow balling up in their hooves. But she was sure nobody would have the time, let alone the inclination, to go riding with her on the very day of the party. If she even suggested it, her brothers would probably have a field day teasing her about her one-track mind. So she might as well close her eyes, go back to sleep—

"Everybody up for breakfast! Stevie! Chad! Alex! Michael! Time to eat!"

Stevie scowled at her aunt's cheery tone. Normally she would have been happy to join the breakfast feast, but the idea of another pre-party meal almost made her lose her appetite. There was a sharp rap on the door, and Aunt Lila poked her head in.

"Seven and a half hours till party time!" she announced.

Stevie sat up in bed and did her best to look enthusiastic. "Wow, not much time left," she said, hoping that her aunt didn't notice the robotlike sound of her voice.

"If you're like Angie, you're probably too excited to eat, but come down anyway and join the crowd, okay, honey?" Aunt Lila urged.

Stevie nodded weakly as her aunt closed the door. "Sure, Aunt Lila. I'll be down right away." Under her breath she added, "Too excited to eat? More like hearing about this party is ruining my appetite!"

Despite Stevie's misgivings, breakfast was a lively affair. The seven cousins squeezed around one table, the three sets of aunts and uncles around another. Everybody put away huge piles of pancakes and bacon. Even Angie mentioned how good the food tasted—instead of describing party hors d'oeuvres for the millionth time.

Stevie found herself enjoying the sibling sparring that her brothers initiated the minute there was a pause in the conversation. "Boy, it's almost eleven A.M. and Stevie hasn't mentioned horses yet," Chad remarked.

"That's because she can't talk with her mouth full," Alex practically yelled. The two of them snorted with laughter.

"Yes: Unlike some people at the table, I actually *have* manners," Stevie shot back happily.

Before her brothers could respond, both tables fell silent to listen to Uncle Chester read the newspaper's weather report. "Continued snow, temperatures in the mid-twenties, slightly warmer tomorrow."

"Tomorrow? Who cares about tomorrow?" Angie demanded.

At the adults' table, Aunt Lila and Uncle Chester had

a quiet word together. They looked concerned, especially since it had already started to snow again. "The caterer has a wedding upstate this morning. She's supposed to get here an hour or two before the guests start coming. It could be tight with the icy roads," said Aunt Lila.

"Oh, please, Mother," Angie jumped in. "The woman is an expert. That's why we're paying her so much. She knows how much time she needs to set up. I'm sure she'll make it."

Stevie glanced at her watch. The time made her grin. They had actually managed to stop talking about the party for thirty-five minutes—a weekend record.

After breakfast, Stevie managed to excuse herself from watching Angie try on outfits. She wandered out to the barn and played with the horses for a while. Back inside the house, she looked around the family room, wondering what she could do to kill the next few hours. Several games were stacked beside the television. Stevie pulled out the Monopoly set and went to see if she could interest Chad and Alex.

"Monopoly?" Alex asked disdainfully. "You think we have time for a game, Stevie? Please. We have to report to Uncle Chester in five minutes."

"Don't tell me. It's something for the party," Stevie guessed.

"That's right. We're helping rearrange the furniture," Chad replied.

"Shouldn't you be helping Aunt Lila with something?" Alex asked suspiciously.

"Yeah, or Angie?" Chad demanded. "She's probably very nervous right now and needs everyone to pitch in."

Stevie stared at the two of them, speechless. Things had gotten out of control. How was she supposed to "pitch in" when her aunt and uncle had hired professionals for every element of the party? Alex and Chad seemed to think she should follow Angie around like a dog, lapping up party talk.

Leaving the boys, she stomped down the hall to the guest room, which she was now sharing with Angie's two little cousins. Luckily the room was empty. Ginny and Beth were probably downstairs counting candles for the birthday cake. Stevie flopped down on her bed, closed her eyes, and tried to think of the most soothing and relaxing thing she could. Pine Hollow Stables. Her beloved Belle and Samson and all the other Pine Hollow horses. No relatives or caterers or high-school bands. A place where nobody cared about Angela Lake's sweet sixteen birthday party. "If only I were there . . . ," Stevie murmured into her pillow.

*　　　*　　　*

"IF ONLY SHE were here!" Lisa exclaimed.

"I know. If there's one brain we could use right now, it's Stevie's. She could probably figure out a way to sneak up on Samson with these stirrups and surprise him into not minding them," Carole agreed with a sigh.

Although Carole spoke lightly, Lisa caught the anxious tone in her voice. All morning, Carole had been preoccupied. Lisa was sure that she was beginning to feel desperate about the situation. The two of them had racked their brains a dozen times trying to figure out what they were doing wrong. Obviously, pretending to think like Stevie was no substitute for the real thing. Nothing they'd tried had made one bit of difference. Samson was in such a playful mood that he had acted up before he even saw the saddle. He'd been prancing from the moment they'd taken him out of his stall.

Lisa figured that at first Samson hadn't liked the stirrups, probably because they were new and strange. So he had acted up. But once he'd seen that he could get away with being silly, he didn't want to stop. Now he did whatever he wanted—pranced, pulled, balked, bucked— the works. Although Carole persisted in calling it the "stirrup problem," Lisa knew it was becoming much more of an all-around training problem.

Usually, when Lisa felt stuck at some point in a

horse's training, she talked it over with Carole and Stevie. Carole's wide experience and profound understanding of horses combined with Stevie's innovative, problem-solving mind almost always helped her figure out a new approach. Now that Stevie was gone and Carole seemed stumped, Lisa felt confused about how to proceed. Maybe when Stevie got back things would look up, but she wasn't even sure about that. Samson was beginning to be downright bratty.

A voice at the door to the ring interrupted Lisa's thoughts. "Hi, girls. How's it going?"

Lisa and Carole spun around to find Max peering in at them.

"F-fine," Carole managed to get out. She was utterly taken aback to see Max there. Even though he looked friendly and interested, it almost seemed to her that he was spying on them. "I thought you were going to a dressage show this weekend," she said nervously.

"That was yesterday," Max explained. "It was only a one-day show."

"How did your students do?" Lisa inquired, with a touch of Stevie-like inspiration. She figured the longer she could keep Max talking about the show, the better. Then maybe he would forget to ask about Samson again. Out of the corner of her eye, she could see Carole trying to get the colt to stand still.

"They did well. We didn't embarrass ourselves, and a few of the students did even better than that."

"Oh? Did they win any ribbons?" Lisa asked.

"Yeah, we brought home a couple of fourths and a sixth." Max paused and turned to look at Carole and Samson. Frantically Lisa tried to think up another question, but she blanked.

"Well, I can see you're busy, so I'll leave you to your devices," Max said.

Lisa let out the breath she was holding. Maybe it was all in her imagination—maybe Max just wanted to say hi.

"Great," Carole said. "We'll see you later."

"But first let's see what you've been doing with Samson," Max finished. He stepped into the ring authoritatively.

Lisa felt her heart sink. She didn't dare look at Carole's face. "We've, uh, been taking it pretty slowly," she said cautiously as Carole walked Samson forward. "We didn't want to rush him, you know."

"Of course not," Max replied, his eyes on the colt.

After a couple of steps, Samson snorted and then dug his toes in. Carole clucked loudly. "Come on, Samson. Wa-alk, wa-alk. Good boy, walk on," she chirped.

In response, Samson lunged forward, stopped dead

again, and reached his head around to nip at the sides of the saddle in annoyance.

"How long has he been doing that?" Max asked.

"Doing what?" said Lisa, feigning innocence.

"Biting at the saddle like that."

"Oh, that," she replied with relief. "Only since this morning. It's one of his newer—" All at once Lisa stopped herself, realizing how terrible what she'd said sounded. She had just admitted to Max that Samson was developing *new* bad habits.

Max nodded and said nothing more while Carole attempted to lead Samson in a circle. The colt bowed away from her playfully. When she came around again, Max motioned her over. Lisa didn't dare say anything. She waited while Max cleared his throat.

"Girls, I wanted to tell you that I appreciate all the time you've been putting in with the colt, but—"

"But he's not usually this bad!" Carole interrupted with a cry.

"She's right, Max. By the end of yesterday, he was working well," Lisa chimed in. She didn't bother to add that by that point they'd taken both the saddle and bridle off.

Max half smiled at the girls' fervent responses. Then he cleared his throat again. "Listen, what I'm about to say has nothing to do with you. That might be hard to understand right now, but it's true. It's just that Mr. Grover happens to be swinging by tonight to pick up a horse a couple of miles down the road, so I've arranged for him to get Samson at the same time. If you want to say good-bye to him, you can bandage him and load him onto the van when it comes."

Carole stared in shock as she struggled to catch her breath. She hadn't heard what Max said past the word "tonight." It just couldn't be true! How could he take Samson away from his home just like that?

"Max, please! We'll work with him all the time. We'll come in the mornings before school—" Carole cried.

Max put a hand up to stop her plea. "Carole, my mind is made up. Samson belongs at Mr. Grover's right now. And you two have been spending too much time away from your own horses as it is. I don't think I've seen you two on Starlight and Prancer in days, have I? Besides," he added, dropping his voice to a gentler tone, "it's not simply a question of how much time you put in."

Carole couldn't answer. Her face burned and her throat felt tight. She was afraid she was going to burst into tears any minute, and she clenched her hands trying to keep them back. There was only one solution: They had to find a way to get Samson past his stirrup problem *right away*. She swallowed hard. The minute Max left the ring, she turned to Lisa. "We'll solve it right now. We have to," she urged.

Lisa looked at her searchingly. "Carole, you know that in a couple of hours we can't—" she began.

"Look, Lisa, are you with me or not?" Carole demanded in a strangled voice.

Lisa stared at Carole, completely taken aback. She had never seen her friend look so upset. Carole's face was heated, and she obviously wanted to cry. But the strangest thing was the panicked look in her eyes. In her heart of hearts, Lisa knew it was a lost cause. But she couldn't desert her friend—not when Carole looked so fragile that she might break any minute. "I'm with you, Carole," she said quietly.

"Lisa, you won't regret it. We can keep Cobalt here where he belongs," Carole responded eagerly.

Lisa paused for a second to see if Carole would realize her slip and correct "Cobalt" to "Samson." When she didn't, Lisa put a comforting arm around her friend. "Sure, Carole," she said. "We'll do the best we can." *But*, she wondered, *what will Carole do if we fail?*

BY THE TIME the Lake clan reassembled for a late lunch at half past one, the snow was coming down thick and fast. From her bedroom window Stevie had noticed the flakes changing size and shape. Now they were small and dense, filling the air with a solid whiteness. It was the kind of snow that made great snowmen. "As if anyone would want to go outside and do something fun," Stevie muttered as she went to join the others.

Downstairs, everybody was making last-minute preparations. Stevie's parents had made lunch, but even though all the relatives were squeezed into the kitchen, the pile of sandwiches remained untouched.

"All right, so the flowers are here, and the furniture's set," Aunt Lila was saying when Stevie entered the room. She held a clipboard and was making check marks on a sheet of paper. "What about the silverware? Is it polished? And Chester, did you get out the big punch bowl for the dining room table?"

"Not yet, we—" Uncle Chester started to say.

"Phew!" Angie hung up the phone, interrupting. "That was the caterer. She's right on schedule."

"Really? That's good news," Stevie's mother chimed in. "Especially with the weather. Do you think—"

"Mother, the silverware!" Angie exclaimed, picking up a knife. "It's green!"

"It's all right, dear—don't worry. Ginny and Beth will start right away. Here, kids, take these rags and the polish and sit right here—"

"Lila, listen," Uncle Chester burst in. "I was going to tell you we can't *find* the punch bowl. We'll have to use pitchers instead."

"Pitchers? Are you kidding, Dad? No way! We have to find it!" Angie wailed.

"We'll go look," Chad volunteered, elbowing Alex.

"Okay, boys. Check in the back of the attic. It should be wrapped in—"

"Honey, I already looked in the attic," Uncle Chester interrupted.

78

"Mom! Ginny punched me!" Beth wailed.

"That's because she pulled my hair!" Ginny countered. The two of them simultaneously burst into tears.

"Hey, wait a minute! Did anyone iron my dress?" Angie cried.

"You were supposed to do that yourself, dear," said Aunt Lila.

"What? You never told me that! I—"

"Angie," snapped her father, "you know better than to talk to your mother like that! If you can't . . ."

Standing in a corner of the room, Stevie smiled. She wasn't sure exactly why, but somehow she was reminded of the time her parents had taken her to see the three-ring circus that came to Washington, D.C., every year. "Do you think anyone will mind if I just grab a sandwich and head out?" she said aloud, to no one in particular. There wasn't even a second's pause in the party-conversation din. "Ah, good. I'll take that as an okay. Let's see, what should I have? This ham-and-cheese on rye looks good." Stevie selected a sandwich, wrapped it in a napkin, and turned to go. "All right, if anyone wants me, I'll be in the barn," she said. Nobody responded. "Right. See you later, then," Stevie added. She had always wondered what it would be like to be invisible; suddenly she knew.

Grabbing her coat from the front hall, she headed out

79

for the small stable. Normally Stevie loved to be in the thick of things when there was excitement in the air, but in this case, her help didn't seem to be needed or wanted. The best thing to do would be to keep out of the way until the party had gotten going—and, come to think of it, maybe even during it. Maybe she should stay outside the whole night.

It was funny, though: Once Stevie had greeted the horses again and taken each of them out for a quick grooming, she was almost ready to head back in. She told herself it was because she was so cold—she still wasn't used to the New Jersey weather, and she'd forgotten to take a hat and gloves with her—but the truth was, although Stevie was horse-crazy, she wasn't used to hanging out in a stable for hours doing nothing. Or at least, not by herself. If Carole and Lisa had been there, the three of them could have thought of games or made up stories or just talked. But without them, Stevie soon began to feel bored and slightly lonely. Carole probably could have camped out alone at the barn without even noticing the time going by, but Stevie thrived on social interaction. She missed people when she was alone for too long. Looking through the stable window back at the house, she wished she could be more involved with the party, but she didn't know how.

"I'll give it one more try," Stevie said to Sparkles,

giving the palomino a good pat. "There must be something *almost* fun that I can do." She tossed all three horses some hay, checked their water, and closed the barn door on the cozy scene.

Outside, there was no question about it: The storm had hit, and the snow was sticking. Even in the hour she'd been with the horses, a couple more inches had accumulated. The trees were beginning to bow down beneath the weight, and a good layer coated the mailbox and the cars parked in the Lakes' driveway.

"You should see it out there," Stevie commented when she joined her parents back in the kitchen. Her mother was busy folding cloth napkins and nodded absently.

"Watch that you don't track any snow into the living room," Mr. Lake advised. He was struggling with a huge bouquet of flowers wrapped in florist paper, a pair of scissors, and two vases.

Stevie sighed and headed upstairs. If she was lucky, her parents would return to earth tomorrow. For now she could see she was going to have to put up with their alien substitutes.

In the second floor hallway Angie had gotten out the iron and ironing board and was attempting to press her dress. "The snow's really coming down," Stevie announced.

81

"Actually, it's not as heavy as before," Angie corrected her. "The minute there's a lull, the plows will come clear the roads."

Stevie was about to protest but decided against it. If Angie wanted to believe the snow was lightening up, why should Stevie worry her more?

"Look, Angie, is there anything I can do?" Stevie asked.

Angie looked up briefly and surveyed Stevie's appearance. "Just make sure you're out of the shower by five-thirty, okay? I'm going to need at least an hour in the bathroom."

"No problem," Stevie replied. She was glad that her mother had made her pack a skirt since the party was going to be so fancy, but she didn't see any need to spend hours getting ready.

For the next half hour, Stevie wandered around the house looking for things she could do to help and trying to get one of the adults to notice the snow. Nobody paid attention to her. They were all too busy with the tasks Aunt Lila had given them. Stevie was now so bored she wanted to scream. On her way up from the basement, where Uncle Chester and her father were digging out card tables, a red plastic sled hanging on the wall caught her eye. She thought of the perfect new snow outside. It was too much to resist. She seized the sled and went to find her brothers. "I'll *make* them come with me," she vowed.

All three of the boys were sharing a third-floor room. Stevie could barely hide her disgust when she saw what they were doing. Michael was lying on one of the beds watching Chad and Alex try on different shirts to see which ones looked the best.

"Getting ready for the cheerleaders?" Stevie asked snidely.

"Getting ready to clean some stalls?" Chad countered, pointing at the hay in Stevie's hair.

"Yeah, you sure smell like it," Alex laughed.

"You smell like you just took a bath in Dad's after-shave," Stevie replied.

Alex smirked. "I guess you wouldn't appreciate it since Phil probably always smells like horses, too."

"For your information—" Stevie began.

"Hey," Michael asked suddenly, "are you going sledding?"

Stevie gave her youngest brother a huge grin. She hadn't known how to finish her sentence, since the truth was Phil *did* smell like horses a lot. But Michael had saved her from having to come up with a good retort. "Yup. Want to come?"

Michael nodded eagerly. *Thank goodness for little brothers who haven't discovered girls*, Stevie thought. Michael probably felt just as left out as she did, with Chad and Alex acting girl-crazy and nobody his age to play with.

The afternoon was perfect for sledding. Stevie and Michael bundled up and went out to the hill behind the house. They sledded down and walked up countless times, until they were exhausted. Then they made snow angels and started on a snowman. They gave up when it started getting dark and the snow began to fall even harder. They ran to the house, flushed and happy. It was the first time in a while that Stevie had had so much fun with one of her brothers.

Unfortunately, the warm glow lasted about two seconds. Inside, the morning chaos had evolved into afternoon hysteria. From what Stevie gathered, the caterer was almost an hour late and hadn't called to say where she was or when she would be coming. The band hadn't arrived, either; and to make matters worse, TV and radio stations were advising people not to leave their houses or drive anywhere unless absolutely necessary. In her now ironed black dress, Angie was sitting on the sofa in the living room surrounded by well-meaning relatives who were trying to comfort her.

"I'm sure the caterer will be here as soon as she can. She probably hasn't called because she doesn't want to take the time to stop," Peg Davison said.

Frowning, Angie folded her hands over her chest. "Or

she hasn't called because she's stuck in the storm and can't get near a phone," she retorted.

"Honey, Aunt Peggy is only trying to help," Angie's mother told her.

"I know, but all I can think of is how humiliated I'm going to be if all my friends show up and there's no party!" Angie wailed. "I've spent the last month at school telling everyone how great it's going to be!"

"I'm sure your friends will understand," Stevie's mother said.

"You don't know my friends, Aunt Catherine!" Angie cried.

At that, Stevie had to stifle a grin. It sounded as if she'd been right about her cousin's football-team and cheerleading friends. If they were the kind of people who would make fun of someone because a snowstorm had ruined her party, they weren't real friends at all. Carole and Lisa, Phil and A.J.—even Betsy Cavanaugh—would have cracked up at the situation. They all would have been good sports and had fun—maybe even more fun—without a caterer or a band.

At that moment, the doorbell rang, interrupting Stevie's thoughts. "I'll get it!" Angie fairly shouted, jumping up. "It's got to be the caterer!"

"Careful in those high heels!" Aunt Lila called after her.

Stevie followed her cousin at a safe distance. After hearing so much about it, she was curious to see the famous caterer's food. But when Angie swung open the door, four bedraggled, snow-covered boys stood on the front steps.

"Uh, hi," one of them said nervously.

Angie's face went from hope to disappointment to annoyance. "It's only you?" she demanded. "Well, at least the band is here. I guess that's better than nothing."

Standing a few steps back, Stevie almost snorted. She couldn't believe her cousin could be so rude! Especially when she was supposed to be best friends with everyone coming.

The boys looked at one another uncomfortably. "Gee, sorry," said another of them.

"Never mind," Angie snapped. "Where are your instruments?"

There was a long, awkward pause. Finally the first boy explained. "Well, you see, our van broke down in a drift about a mile away, and we barely made it here on foot."

"Yeah, we didn't have a hat for Capuano here, and he's getting frostbite on his ears," another boy added.

"Excuse me? *You don't have your instruments?*" Angie said, her voice as icy cold as the air blowing in the door.

For one awful minute she stared at them, enraged. Then she shrieked, turned on her high heels, and fled.

Stevie would have laughed had she not been so embarrassed. Instead she stood there, speechless at her cousin's behavior.

"Uh, hi," said the boy again. "We're Voyager. I'm Ted, and this is Mike, Jeff, and Kevin."

"Hi!" Stevie said back, recovering herself. Angie was right about one thing: The boys were definitely good-looking. "I mean, come in—you must be frozen."

"Practically," said the boy.

"I'm Stevie, by the way."

"Oh, my gosh, you poor things," Aunt Lila said, coming up behind Stevie to see what the commotion was. In a flash she had the boys inside and was handing Stevie a pile of coats to spread out on the laundry-room drying rack.

When Stevie rejoined the group a few minutes later, all four boys were seated around the kitchen table while Stevie's mother fed them sandwiches and Aunt Lila made hot chocolate. Before long, the boys started to lose their worried looks and relax and enjoy themselves. Stevie decided to do her part to help cheer them up by telling some awful old jokes. "Hey, everybody! What's black and white and red all over?"

"A newspaper!" one of the boys called.

Stevie shook her head. "Nope. It's a skunk with poison ivy."

The boys groaned. "That's almost as bad as my knock-knock," Ted volunteered.

"I seriously doubt that," Stevie challenged him.

"All right. Knock-knock," Ted said.

"Who's there?" Stevie asked.

"Orange."

"Orange who?"

"Orange you glad you're you?"

Everyone at the table howled. Then all of the boys started vying to tell their own stupid jokes.

For the first time all weekend, Stevie began to think the party might not be so boring after all. *If there is a party*, she thought, looking out the window at the snow.

IT WASN'T LONG before the guests started trickling in. Every few minutes or so the doorbell rang, and Angie kept running to answer it. Without getting too involved, Stevie kept an eye on the proceedings. Angie, who'd been given a lecture by her parents, managed to greet the guests almost politely, but Stevie noticed her crestfallen look every time somebody who wasn't the caterer arrived.

First a handful of girls from the cheerleading squad came. They were wearing boots with their nice dresses and carrying their shoes in bags. "Angie!" one of them shrieked. "You must be a wreck! We didn't even know if the party was still on."

"We made Val's mom drive us over anyway," another girl piped up.

"That's right. We weren't about to miss the bash we've been hearing about all month," said the third one.

Angie smiled wanly. "Oh, good. I'm glad you could make it," she said, her voice little more than a whisper.

Out of nowhere, Chad and Alex appeared in the hall. "Here, Angie, we'll show these girls in. You go and relax."

"Relax? Are you kidding!" Angie sputtered. Then the doorbell rang again, and Stevie's brothers whisked the cheerleaders away.

It was the Lakes' next-door neighbors, the Kellys. They had walked over with flashlights. "Gosh, it's dark out there," Mr. Kelly said.

"It sure is. I hope you're stocked up with candles and flashlights and kerosene in case the lights go," Mrs. Kelly added. Stevie caught Angie's horrified look as the couple took off their coats and disappeared into the back of the house.

A little while later someone showed up in snowshoes. It was Angie's English teacher, the only teacher she'd invited. "I didn't want to risk the drive so I came over in these," the gray-haired man explained.

"Thanks for coming, Mr. Scott," Angie said, her voice lackluster.

Mr. Scott disappeared into the house, reciting Robert Frost's "Stopping By Woods on a Snowy Evening" as he went.

A few more hearty guests arrived in four-wheel-drive vehicles, on cross-country skis, or simply on foot. By eight o'clock, the kitchen was packed. Almost all of the guests had gravitated to the room and were busy putting away mugs of hot chocolate and whatever food Angie's parents had managed to dig up. Three or four large guys who Stevie decided had to be football players volunteered to shovel the stone path up to the house.

Meanwhile the phone was practically ringing off the hook. Stevie's mother, who was guarding the receiver, had to keep shaking her head at the question on Angie's face: No caterer—just another guest canceling because of the weather. When a report came over the radio saying the snow would continue all night, it was the last straw for the birthday girl. Angie burst into tears and sat crying in the living room, trails of black mascara and eyeliner running down her face.

Not knowing what to say, Stevie perched on the window seat watching different people come in to try to comfort her cousin. Her mother tried, then Chad and Alex, then the Davison kids, then Michael, then Uncle Chester. But Angie just cried harder.

At first Stevie couldn't help feeling a bit smug. After all the planning, it looked as if the party was going to be a huge disaster. Probably the New Jersey Lakes—and especially Angie—had cursed it by worrying about every last detail so much. Now they would learn their lesson. But then Stevie felt a pang of guilt. Something in her reasoning wasn't right. Just then Chad walked by with a couple of cheerleaders. Stevie tried to think up something she could say to tease him, but Chad beat her to it.

"I'm giving Brenda and Diane a tour around the house now," he said happily. Then he whispered to Stevie, "Maybe you could show them the manure pile later—I know it's your favorite spot."

Stevie made a face. Chad had never gotten over the fact that at Pony Club rallies the stable management judges even examined manure piles to make sure they were up to their standards. But that was Pony Club: Every last detail was—Stevie clapped a hand over her mouth. How could she have been so blind? Of *course* something in her reasoning was wrong! She had been annoyed at Angie all weekend not because she was discussing and planning every last detail but because she was discussing and planning every last detail *for a party*! If Angie had been getting ready for a show, Stevie would have been the first to agonize with her over what color breeches she would wear and what food the horses would eat, and to review the classes one by one.

There was no denying that Angie's priorities had changed from horses to clothes, cheerleading, and boys. But the truth was Stevie had been so disappointed by the change that she hadn't been able to see the parallel between planning for a Pony Club event and planning for a social event. When she thought about it, it wasn't surprising that Angie pursued her new interests with the same single-mindedness that had once made her so successful in the show ring.

Even more importantly, no matter what Angie liked to do with her time, she was still family and always would be.

"Hey, Angie?" Stevie said quietly.

"What?" came a choked response.

"You know, I was thinking, even though some people are canceling, your family's almost all here, and so are most of your close friends, aren't they?"

Angie nodded dully, her eyes on the living room floor.

"And even if there won't be live music, a couple of the guys in the band said they would deejay with the stereo."

Angie nodded again.

"So all we have to do is wait for the caterer. I'm sure she'll come," Stevie predicted, crossing her fingers. "In fact, that's probably her now," she added, hearing the phone ring again.

But no sooner were the words out of her mouth than Aunt Lila appeared in the doorway, her face grave. "Angela, that was the caterer."

Angie immediately sat up straight. "And?" she asked breathlessly.

"I—I'm sorry, honey. She's completely snowed in, in a town thirty miles away."

For a second the room was too still. Then the storm burst. Angie flung her head against the couch and began to bawl. Absolutely hysterical, she sobbed and cried and gulped for air and sobbed some more. The sound brought Uncle Chester running. When he noticed how distraught Angie was, he and Aunt Lila exchanged urgent words.

"Look, I'm telling you there's practically no food in the house. We cleared out the refrigerator to make room for all the stuff the caterer was supposed to bring," Stevie heard Uncle Chester say.

"There must be something," Aunt Lila whispered.

"Yes: half a box of stale crackers, some coffee, and a

large assortment of condiments on the refrigerator door," Uncle Chester replied drily.

"What'll we do? We can't send people away after they've made such an effort to get here!"

"I'll have to take the van and drive to the supermarket and buy some food there. It should still be open," said Uncle Chester, with a quick glance at the clock on the mantelpiece.

"What about the roads?" Aunt Lila asked.

"The plow's just been by—they should be all right."

When they'd finished talking, Angie's parents announced the plan. "It's the only solution, honey," Aunt Lila said.

Once again, Stevie tried to help calm her cousin down. She took Angie up to the bathroom to wash her face and redo her makeup. Then the two girls went back down to join the others.

By now the mood in the kitchen was downright jovial. Sitting in a circle on the floor, the kids were playing a huge game of I Doubt It while the adults stood around swapping snowstorm stories. The cheerleaders had borrowed sweatshirts to wear over their dresses and had joined right in.

Once she got Angie settled, Stevie dashed outside to make sure her uncle had gotten away all right. To her surprise, the van was still parked in the exact same spot in the driveway, covered in snow. "Uncle Chester?" Stevie called.

"I'm here," a voice called back. Then a bundled-up figure carrying a shovel emerged from around the side of the van. "I'm here," Uncle Chester repeated, "and I don't think I'll be leaving any time soon."

"Why? What's wrong?" Stevie asked.

Uncle Chester pointed to a huge snowbank behind the van. "The plows came through, all right. They dumped that huge pile of snow there and blocked the driveway. I've been trying to get at it with the shovel, but it's rock solid. In fact, I wouldn't be surprised if there were some *real* rocks in there. It's too heavy to move."

Stevie scanned the driveway anxiously. "Could you take the station wagon?" she asked.

Uncle Chester shook his head. "The van is our only car with snow tires on it. I just can't risk the wagon in this kind of weather . . . even if Angie is disappointed," he added quietly.

By then, a few of the adult guests had gathered at the door. "Anything I can do to help?" asked one of the neighbors.

"Thanks, but unless anybody can get to a car with snow chains, we're stuck," replied Uncle Chester.

Mr. Kelly peered out at the weather. "I could go home

and see about our car," he said after a minute. "It might be okay."

His face thoughtful, Uncle Chester motioned for Stevie to come inside with him. In the hall he slowly took off his coat and hung it up. A few of the other guests halfheartedly offered to drive, but it was obvious that no one relished the idea. Even though the supermarket was less than half a mile away, the roads were looking worse all the time. In the time that had passed since the plowing, snow had begun to accumulate all over again. It would be a treacherous trip.

"We're not going to do anything foolish," Uncle Chester declared, shaking the snow from his boots. "It's too bad about my daughter's party, and we're sorry that you all came out in the storm, but it would be stupid to drive anywhere right now. I'm afraid that's all there is to it."

Mumbling about how sorry they were, the guests started to discuss when it would be safe to leave. Stevie watched them with a sinking feeling. The next time the plow came through, the ones who had driven would run out so they could get home. By then every supermarket in town would be closed, if they weren't already. It looked as if salvaging the party was impossible.

So? Why should I care? Stevie asked herself. But it was no use. The fact was she did care. It made her sad to

97

think that all the party-goers were going to be disappointed, that her aunt and uncle had worked so hard for nothing. But most of all she felt bad for Angie, who would dread going to school when the long weekend was over and having to tell people that the great party hadn't happened. Stevie knew all about talking something up at school only to have a plan backfire.

The worst part was it was out of Angie's control. She hadn't ordered the weather, after all. It was like having a big horse show get rained out after all the practicing, planning, and tack cleaning, after loading the horses and driving there. It was all for nothing if the show got called off. More than once Stevie had been all excited about riding and had had to sit in the van the whole morning while the horses waited, doing nothing.

Suddenly Stevie gasped. For the second time that day, thinking about horses had made a lightbulb go on in her brain. She stood bolt upright. All excited about riding? The horses waiting, doing nothing? Why hadn't she thought of it before?

"Uncle Chester! Uncle Chester! I've got it!" Stevie yelled.

IN A MATTER of minutes, Stevie had filled her uncle in on the plan and dashed out to the barn to saddle Sparkles and Birdie. The horses looked mildly surprised to be getting tacked up instead of fed dinner. "Obviously you boys aren't used to The Saddle Club way of life," Stevie told them, tightening first one girth and then the other.

Grinning with excitement, she thought back over some of the thrilling rides she and Carole and Lisa had taken. They'd saved a movie star (Skye Ransom), a marriage (Max's), and a starring role (Lisa's, in a community theater production of *Annie*), among other things.

"Tonight's ride will be a little different, though," Stevie told the two geldings as she tried to warm both bits in her hands at the same time. "We won't be galloping, and we won't be bareback because we need as many saddlebags as we can carry. All right, Sparkles, open up. Sorry if it's still cold." Like the well-trained horse he was, Sparkles obligingly took the bit. Birdie followed suit, and Stevie led both of them out to the front yard.

Uncle Chester was waiting with improvised saddlebags. Quickly he tied them to the little metal Ds on the saddles' cantles; then he handed Stevie a backpack to wear. A half dozen guests had come out to see them off. "Good luck!" Aunt Lila called.

"Thanks!" said Stevie. She mounted easily and waved to the group at the door. Then they headed Sparkles and Birdie down the driveway and out onto the road. Although they couldn't trot on the snowy pavement, the horses kept up a good walking pace through the steadily falling snow.

"I sure am thankful for these streetlamps," Uncle Chester remarked. "Without them, it would be pitch dark."

"Yeah, we'd have to use Sparkles' mane for light," Stevie joked, noticing how the palomino's white crest gleamed with snow.

Figuring out a solution—and one that involved horses—had put Stevie in the best mood she'd been in all weekend. She felt exuberant riding through the snowy night on an important mission. It would make a great story to tell Carole and Lisa—providing it worked. The one worrisome thing was that as Stevie and her uncle rode into town, they passed a few shops that were closed. The dark, quiet Main Street was like a deserted ghost town.

"You do think the supermarket will be open, don't you, Uncle Chester?" Stevie asked anxiously.

Uncle Chester frowned. "I hope so. It's supposed to stay open for another half hour, but you never know, with the weather this bad."

A little farther down the road, Stevie noticed that the lights were on at the local gas station's Quickie Mart. That was a good sign. She patted Sparkles and crossed her fingers. It would be terrible to have to go home after their dramatic departure and face Angie's disappointment. Besides, Stevie was excited about the party now, too.

Before she could fret any longer, they turned into the parking lot of the supermarket. Stevie's heart sank to the bottom of her cowboy boots. Except for a couple of cars that seemed to have been left there for the night, the lot was empty. And the store was dark. Stevie urged Sparkles closer. There was a sign hanging in the window that told the worst: CLOSED DUE TO WEATHER.

Uncle Chester drew Birdie alongside Sparkles. Stevie heard him sigh loudly. "Well, Stevie, we've done our best. Aunt Lila and I will just have to try to reschedule this party for another time. Let's head home now and break the news."

Stevie nodded absently. Her mind was whirling. Something told her she couldn't give up now. There had to be somewhere they could get their hands on some food. Then she had it. She wheeled Sparkles and led the way out of the parking lot and back down the street toward home.

"Stevie?" Uncle Chester called, following on Birdie. "Was it something I said?"

Stevie didn't have time to respond. They had reached their destination: the Quickie Mart at the gas station. The owner was inside, but he was turning off the lights! Jumping off Sparkles, Stevie tossed the reins at her uncle. "Hold him for one minute while I talk to the guy!" she called over her shoulder.

When she tried the front door, it was locked. She rattled the handle and rapped on the glass until the man came to the door and opened it. "Look, I'm just about to close so that I don't get snowed in here," he said.

"Please can we just have five minutes—no, two minutes! If you're stranded, I'll give you a ride home," Stevie begged.

The man's eyebrows shot up. "You don't look old enough to drive, young lady," he said, surprised.

"No—I mean a ride on a horse," Stevie explained. She stood aside and pointed to Sparkles, Birdie, and Uncle Chester.

The man did a double take. "You mean to tell me you *rode* here?" he demanded.

Stevie nodded, crossing her fingers for the millionth time that night.

"I thought I saw a couple of horses go by a few minutes ago, but I said to myself, 'Jim, you're either crazy or hallucinating or an old fool or all three!' But I'll be darned—I was right."

Stevie had crept and sidled her way halfway inside the store by the time the man finished talking. "So does that mean we can come in?" she pleaded.

"Seeing that you're my first customers ever on horseback, I guess it does," he decided.

Stevie didn't need a second invitation. She ran to Uncle Chester, helped him tie the horses to a sign next to the side of the building, and bolted for the door again.

Inside Jim had snapped the lights back on. Uncle

Chester greeted him and thanked him briefly while Stevie began tearing around grabbing food. Soon she and her uncle were tossing bags of chips and boxes of cookies at the counter. "One bag of sour cream and onion!" Stevie cried, keeping a running total of the take. "Two bags of barbecue! Three nachos—hey, is there any salsa?"

Uncle Chester scanned the shelves. "No salsa, but there's spray-cheese in a can! For cookies we've got chocolate chip, Oreos, peanut butter . . ."

Before long the counter was piled high with all kinds of soda and junk food. Stevie added a dozen candy bars, which they could use for prizes, and then glanced around to make sure they hadn't missed anything. Hanging behind the counter was a big color poster—a huge submarine sandwich.

Jim, the owner, followed her glance. "It's kind of late to be making hoagies . . ."

Remembering that in Philadelphia they called subs "hoagies," Stevie launched into an all-out appeal. "Oh, please! You don't understand—it's my cousin's sweet sixteen, only it's not that sweet because the caterer couldn't come and all of the cheerleaders and football players and the band and neighbors and relatives are at the house with nothing to eat and a couple of three-foot subs—er, hoagies—would save the whole party!"

Jim seemed totally bowled over by Stevie's speech. "Well, okay, I guess," he said.

"Yea!" Stevie clapped her hands together in delight. Jim got out bread and a bunch of cold cuts and condiments and whipped up two three-footers. Getting into the spirit of things, the man even helped them carry all of the food out to the horses. Everything fit in the saddlebags and backpacks except for the sandwiches. Uncle Chester and Stevie decided they could each hold one while they rode. They mounted, and Jim carefully passed up the hoagies. Before leaving, Uncle Chester made sure that Jim's car would start.

"Thanks again. You really saved my daughter's birthday," said Chester.

"And you gave me the best story I've had in ages. Two customers come to a gas station—on horseback—and buy everything in the store! I guess you didn't want to fill them up with unleaded, did you?" Jim joked, waving good-bye.

The ride back seemed to take forever. Stevie held the reins with one hand, western-style, and balanced the sub across the pommel of the saddle with the other. Uncle Chester did the same. Neither of them spoke—it was too nerve-racking to try to make conversation. After what seemed like an eternity, they could make out the lights of the house down the road.

They could also see two figures coming toward them on cross-country skis.

"Who on earth would be skiing at a time like this?" Uncle Chester asked.

Stevie squinted hard. "Chad and Alex Lake, naturally," she answered.

"We came to see if you'd gotten lost in the storm," Alex explained cheerfully.

"I hate to disappoint you, but I'm alive and well," Stevie said, grinning at the welcome sight of her two brothers. "Say, Uncle Chester—these two look like they could use a couple of sandwiches, don't they?"

"They sure do," Uncle Chester agreed.

He and Stevie passed off their three-footers to Chad and Alex, both of whom looked slightly surprised at the size of the "couple of sandwiches."

"Take them up to the house while we unload, okay? Sneak them into the kitchen and have Mom slice them up so we can put everything out at once," Stevie instructed, guessing that they were too hungry to protest. Sure enough, Chad and Alex did as they were told without any fuss.

In the front yard of the house, Stevie and her uncle dismounted. They led the horses back to the barn, scraped the snow off their coats, blanketed them, and fed them. Stevie would have liked to linger with the

106

horses, but she knew they had to hurry back to the house with the bags of food.

Pausing on the doorstep before they went in, Uncle Chester put his hand out for Stevie to give him a high five. "Great thinking, Stevie," he said. "Angie's going to be so happy."

"I hope so," Stevie replied. She had just remembered the list of groceries Angie had pressed into her hand before they had left. She drew it out of her jacket pocket, but it was a sodden, snowy mess. Anyway, Stevie doubted that the Quickie Mart would have had any of Angie's requests.

"Hello-o! We're home!" Uncle Chester called, pushing through the door. Stevie followed him, laden with bags.

Angie immediately appeared in the hallway. Despite the new, casual tone of the party, she had redone her hair and reapplied her powder, lipstick, and mascara so that her face was perfectly madeup again. "Phew! I was getting nervous. Everyone's been really nice, but I can tell they're all ravenous. Now, did you find the smoked salmon and the Belgian endive and the other things on the list?"

Stevie looked her cousin boldly in the eye. "Not exactly," she said. She handed Angie one of the bags. "But come on. Let's get this party started!"

11

As SLOWLY AS she could, Lisa walked down the aisle. She and Carole had taken a break from the training to groom Prancer and Starlight, but they'd agreed to meet back in Samson's stall. Lisa was already five minutes late; she couldn't put it off any longer. The way she was dragging her feet, though, they could have been made of concrete. She was dreading what she was sure would be the final session with the colt, dreading Carole's reaction when they failed again.

Stopping at every stall along the way, Lisa greeted the

school horses and ponies, gave Belle a special pat for Stevie, and dawdled over Delilah.

"You're his mother, Delilah," Lisa murmured to the palomino mare. "Can't you tell us what to do?"

Delilah placidly chewed a bite of hay, staring dreamily into space. "Thanks," Lisa said. "Thanks a lot, Mom."

Inching down the aisle, Lisa thought how much easier it would have been if equine mothers trained their foals. In one sense, they did—the same as all animals. Delilah had taught Samson to take care of himself: to run with her, eat hay and grain, and drink out of a water bucket. She'd also taught him to trust humans, the way she did. But the minute the foal was ready to begin real training, he had been weaned away from his mother.

I wonder what 'stirrup' is in horse language, Lisa mused. She paused in front of Samson's door, listening. "Carole?"

"I'm in here," Carole said quietly.

Lisa opened the stall door slowly. As the light fell on Carole's face, Lisa could see that it was wet and that Carole's eyes were puffy. But Carole looked calmer than she had in days. She was actually smiling through her tears.

"Do you want to take Samson to the indoor?" Lisa asked hesitantly.

109

Carole shook her head. "No, I don't think so."

"Are you sure? We probably still have some time," said Lisa.

Carole swallowed hard. "Yes—time to wrap him and get him ready to go to the Grovers'."

Lisa could hardly believe she'd heard correctly. "Carole, I—I thought—" She stopped, not knowing how to continue.

Carole nodded. "I know. Believe me, I know. You thought I wasn't going to be able to let Samson go. I thought so, too. I came in here to get him a little while ago. I started crying, and I just couldn't stop."

"Carole, I'm sorry," Lisa murmured. She hated to think of her friend crying by herself while she dawdled.

"No, listen. The more I cried, the more I realized I was crying for Cobalt, not Samson. And once I let myself cry about it, I felt much better. I—I know that Samson has to go away because it's best for him."

Lisa hardly knew what to say. She'd been preparing herself for the worst. Instead, Carole had figured everything out on her own. What made it even more difficult to respond was that Lisa knew that Cobalt's death reminded Carole, in some way, of the death of her mother. Carole had lost both of them within a couple of years. Any time she got close to a person or an animal, she was taking a risk that she would face yet another loss. Even

110

something like letting Samson go to Mr. Grover's could trigger her fears. "Oh, Carole," Lisa said finally, "I'm sorry you still miss Cobalt so much."

Carole sighed. "I do miss him," she said honestly. Then she added, in a determined voice, "But I can't make Samson into a replacement for his father. If we keep him here, we'll just be jeopardizing his chances to become a fantastic pleasure horse, right?"

"Right," Lisa echoed her. "And we don't want to do that. So what do you say we give him a good good-bye grooming?" she suggested.

Carole looked pleased by the suggestion. The two girls led the colt out and cross tied him in the aisle. As they curried and brushed him, they chattered and joked happily for the first time in days. When his black coat was gleaming, Lisa got cotton and leg wraps from the tack room. As they were rolling the bandages, they caught sight of Max on his way to his office.

"Max!" Carole waved him over.

"So you're getting Samson ready for his trip?" Max asked. By the tone of his voice, the girls could tell that he knew how important the question was.

Carole took a deep breath. "Yes. I—we—we know we can't cure him of his problems, and he belongs with a professional," she said. Then she looked down, flustered.

Max nodded approvingly. "It's a hard realization to

111

come to, Carole, but I think you'll both agree with me that it's the best," he said seriously.

The way Max spoke sounded like he was addressing them as fellow horsemen. After her desperation over the last few days, Carole felt both humbled and thankful. She'd been afraid that Max would think she'd acted stupidly, but he simply seemed pleased that she and Lisa understood why Samson should go away to be trained.

"When Mr. Grover gets here, I'll want you to fill him in on the colt's training so far," Max continued. "As we've said before, you girls know as much as anyone about his progress."

"Or lack of progress in a couple of areas," Carole kidded, surprised that she could already joke about the dreaded stirrup problem.

"That, too." Max laughed, turning on his heel.

When he was gone, the girls carefully wrapped Samson's legs to protect them on the trip. Seeing the colt all ready to go, Carole felt a pang of sadness come over her.

"Hey, don't forget—it's only for a few months, not forever," Lisa reminded her. "He'll be coming back before you know it." She put a comforting arm around Carole's shoulders.

Carole nodded. "And when he does come back, he'll be as well-trained and obedient as all of Max's horses—a

112

real pleasure to ride, just like his sire was and his dam still is," she said firmly, more to herself than to Lisa.

"Speaking of Delilah, do you remember the day he was born?" Lisa asked. "It was the first time I'd seen a mare foal."

"How could I forget? I was completely obsessed with him then, too!" Carole recalled. Waiting for Mr. Grover to arrive, the two of them reminisced about all the times—fun, remarkable, and challenging—they'd had with Samson.

All too soon, the heavy trailer tires crunched on the driveway. Lisa and Carole looked at each other. It was time to say good-bye, if only for awhile. Together they smothered the colt in hugs. Then Lisa handed the lead line to Carole so that she could load him.

"Hey, look! It snowed!" Lisa exclaimed as the trio emerged from the stable. A light dusting of snow had covered the ground since the morning. Pricking up his ears, Samson rolled his eyes at the white stuff. The girls laughed at the startled expression on his face.

"It's a send-off for Samson from Mother Nature," Carole murmured.

Lisa nodded, dropping back to watch the colt walk forward with Carole.

As she led him toward the trailer, Carole felt her

heart swell with motherly pride. Against the white snow, Samson's black coat looked even more brilliant. He was healthy and well-groomed, and, despite their setbacks, Carole knew that The Saddle Club had contributed immeasurably to his training.

"Is this the horse who wants to come to school at my place?" Mr. Grover inquired. He hopped out of the pickup truck that pulled the trailer to greet them. To Carole's delight, he offered Samson a carrot from his pocket.

"This is the one," Lisa spoke up. "Samson, by Cobalt out of Delilah."

"Well, then, if he's half as good a horse as his mother or father, he'll be one in a million," Mr. Grover predicted. Moving unhurriedly, he let down the ramp of the trailer.

Carole whispered fiercely to her charge. "You'd better load right, now. No funny business." She gave a cluck, and Samson followed her up the ramp like an old hand.

"Nicely done," Mr. Grover remarked. He, Max, and Lisa had gathered in the parking lot for a final word. When Carole joined them, Mr. Grover praised her for the good work she'd put in. "Max tells me you girls are to thank for making my job easier."

Carole and Lisa brushed off the praise. "We're not

being modest," Lisa assured Mr. Grover. "We've had some real problems with him lately."

"Yes, they started when we put stirrups on the saddle he wears . . ." With that, Carole was off and running with one of her notoriously long explanations. Luckily Mr. Grover looked rapt with interest in what she was saying. He countered with an even longer explanation about some possible solutions he would consider trying. Lisa caught the words "natural horsemanship" and smiled. Max couldn't have picked a trainer whom Carole would like more.

When the trailer finally rumbled out of the driveway almost half an hour later, Carole turned to Lisa, a content look on her face. "Mr. Grover's going to be perfect for Samson. But it just hit me—I wish Stevie could have been here to see him off, too. After all, she was there when he was born and through all our other adventures with him. It doesn't seem right that the entire Saddle Club wasn't here to bid him farewell."

Lisa agreed. It really was too bad that Stevie had missed the send-off. She and Carole watched the trailer disappear and then headed wearily into the barn. "But you know what?" Lisa said. "We'll all be together for a much more important moment—the moment when we welcome Samson back to Pine Hollow."

*   *   *

STEVIE CREPT STEALTHILY through the dining room and into the back hallway. She waited a split second outside the bathroom door before flinging it open. "Found you!" she yelled.

"Finally!" said one of the football players. "It was getting crowded in here." One by one, nine people spilled out of the tiny bathroom. They were playing Sardines, and Stevie had been It.

"That's because you've already eaten so much!" said Diane, a cheerleader.

"Did somebody say 'eat'?" Alex asked. Everyone looked at one another and sprinted for the kitchen.

Although it didn't resemble the one Angie had spent so much time planning, the party was finally in full swing. Instead of live music, the band was playing CDs. Instead of caviar canapés, the adults were munching chips and Slim Jims. Instead of a fancy entree, Aunt Lila had served three-foot hoagies. Angie, the reigning party princess, sat at the kitchen table, surrounded by friends.

Angie had been more upset than ever when she'd gotten a look at the Quickie Mart provisions. But then one of the guys from the band had yelled, "Cool! Nacho chips and Cheez Whiz!" Everybody else had followed suit. Even some of the grown-ups had professed addictions to various kinds of junk food. Since nobody else

116

seemed to mind—and once Angie saw that her guests were having fun in spite of all the mishaps—Angie started to have fun, too.

The funniest part about the party was that it was half elegant and half less-than-casual. Some people were in sweats and turtlenecks; others had managed to stay gussied up in dresses and suits. And even though they were eating Quickie Mart hors d'oeuvres, they were eating them with the Lakes' good silverware. The boys had finally located the punch bowl, and Uncle Chester had filled it with Kool-Aid. The cheerleaders didn't seem to mind, though: they let Chad and Alex continue to refill their paper cups.

As for Stevie, she was in heaven. She'd become a sort of master of ceremonies and was coming up with all sorts of games for the guests to play and awarding candy bars to the winners, whether young or old. They'd played Bobbing for Oreos, Pin the Lips on the Fashion Magazine Model, and elimination rounds of the card game Spit; and they'd had blindfolded potato chip taste tests. Then they'd played the killer game of Sardines, which had just ended. Meanwhile there was an ongoing Lake-family trivia quiz, with Stevie's dad and Uncle Chester making up questions and keeping score. Looking around the loud, jammed kitchen, Stevie, for one, was sure that the snowstorm had been a blessing in disguise.

The evening flew by, and soon it was time for the birthday cake. They had to serve it before the guests started to trickle away. Unfortunately, "it"—a three-tiered lemon cake with vanilla icing—was miles away, stranded with the caterer. Stevie noticed her mother and Aunt Lila holding a whispered consultation. "Listen," Stevie told them, "just get everyone out of here for a few minutes, turn out the lights, and get ready to sing. I'll take care of the rest."

The women looked doubtful but followed Stevie's instructions, shooing everyone out of the kitchen to the living room. Stevie dashed around for a few minutes getting organized. Then she found a match and hastily lit the candles. In the dark hush, she paraded out and, with much flair, presented the "cake": sixteen Twinkies, each with a candle stuck in the middle, carefully arranged on Aunt Lila's best silver tray.

The whole party, including Angie, burst into applause at the sight of the improvised cake. Stevie inhaled loudly and began to sing. "Happy birthday to you, happy—"

One of the band members came forward, holding a hand up. "Stevie, you really should leave the singing to the experts," he said. The rest of the band gathered around. "Okay, guys—one, two, three!"

Stevie noticed Angie's jaw drop. Each of the boys had

118

found a makeshift instrument. One held a kazoo, one had Uncle Chester's ukelele, and there was a makeshift percussion section of pots and wooden spoons. They launched into an enthusiastic version of the song and then did a reprise, yelling, "Everybody join in!"

Beaming with delight, Angie blew out all of the candles on her first try.

"Hey, do you guys know 'When Johnnie Comes Marching Home'?" Chad asked.

"Yeah, that's a great American Revolution song!" Stevie cried.

"Uh, that would be a great *Civil War* song," Chad murmured. Stevie put an arm over her forehead and pretended to swoon.

Meanwhile, after a quick consultation, the band struck up the tune. The singing was so much fun that they played another—and another—until all the guests joined the impromptu sing-along. They did songs from musicals like *Oklahoma!* and *Guys and Dolls*, they did popular songs from the radio, and they even threw in a few Christmas carols in honor of the weather.

Angie joined right in, belting with the best of them. Stevie was overjoyed. Her cousin had finally lost her airs and settled back into her old self. And, Stevie had to admit, she'd been completely wrong about Angie's friends. Maybe the cheerleaders would have been more

119

standoffish at an elegant party, but today they had been nothing but fun—not to mention the fact that they'd completely distracted Chad and Alex from doing anything else besides following them around.

As she was musing on the funny way the day had turned out, the music stopped. Stevie looked up expectantly, thinking someone would request another song. Instead, Angie and the three cheerleaders came forward. "Give me an *S!* Give me a *T!* Give me an *E!* Give me a *V!* Give me an *I!* Give me an *E!* What does it spell?" Angie yelled.

"Stevie!" the girls responded. In the space that they had, the four of them did a dance movement that ended in a split. Then they jumped up and surrounded Stevie.

"Three cheers for my cousin Stevie!" Angie yelled.

As the first "Hip, hip, hooray" hit her ears, Stevie thrilled with pride. That was another thing about cheerleaders she hadn't taken into consideration: They could cheer for her!

IT HAD BEEN the longest long weekend that any of The Saddle Club members could remember. "So much has happened since you left, I don't know where to start," Lisa said to Stevie.

All three girls were lazing in the locker room after their Tuesday-afternoon lesson. They knew that Mrs. Reg would catch them any minute and give them tack to clean, but for right now, they just had to catch up. They were also waiting for Max's wife, Deborah, who had promised to pick them up and take them over to see Samson settled in his new home.

"Or, you could say that only one thing happened: Samson left to go and be trained at Mr. Grover's," Carole said with a grin. "It's just that so many things had to happen before *that* happened."

"Right," Lisa agreed. "Like we had to try ninety-nine ways to get Samson used to the stirrups before realizing that nothing we did was going to work."

"Only ninety-nine? Lisa, that's not like you," Stevie kidded. "You're such a perfectionist that I wouldn't have expected you to quit before at least a hundred!"

"Actually, Lisa had the sense to quit, but I didn't," Carole said, more seriously. "I didn't want to feel that I wasn't doing everything I could for Samson, since I hadn't been able to do enough to save Cobalt's life. I was really getting paranoid—I thought Max was spying on us when he was only keeping tabs on Samson like he does on any other horse."

"And I talked to Max yesterday. It really was a coincidence that we ran into problems at the same time that Max was planning to send Samson away. We didn't realize that. To us it looked like we messed up and so Max was taking him away as punishment," Lisa explained.

Lisa and Carole agreed that the main thing they had learned was that sometimes somebody outside The Saddle Club was more qualified or more experienced to do the job at hand. "My dad tried to tell us that, but I, for one, didn't get it," Carole said.

Lisa pointed out that she hadn't gotten it, either, at first. As a top student, she was used to taking on tasks that no one thought she could do and making them come out perfectly. And she shared the we-can-do-any-thing Saddle Club spirit with Stevie and Carole. But, unlike Carole, she hadn't had a bond with Cobalt. So when Samson started misbehaving, she could see that they weren't getting anywhere with his training.

"So, Carole, do you miss Samson a lot already?" Stevie inquired gently.

Carole thought for a minute. "Yes and no," she said finally. "When I walked in today, I thought of his empty stall and I felt sad. But then I felt this overwhelming sense of relief that his training's in Mr. Grover's hands now. I got a good night's sleep last night for the first time since the stirrup problem began. It seems so obvious to me now: Sometimes you've just got to call in the expert."

Stevie grinned. "Experts aren't always the answer, though," she said. She filled her friends in on the week-end, starting with Angie's new personality and ending with the very amateur way the party had turned out, under her guidance.

123

"But you're wrong, Stevie," said Lisa. "If there's anything you're an expert at, it's throwing parties and having fun."

"That's exactly what I was going to say," Carole agreed. "You should hire yourself out to people who don't know how to enjoy themselves."

"I thought my cousin had fallen into that category, but she turned out to be okay. I think part of her attitude problem was that she was incredibly nervous about the party. But once her sweet sixteen turned out well, she was almost a different person." The day after the party, Stevie and Angie had hung out all day. In a lot of ways, Angie really was still the girl Stevie remembered. They'd gone for a long ride, and Angie had been just as enthusiastic about it as Stevie, now that the party was behind her. The two of them had swapped stories about their horses and friends. Because not many girls she knew rode, Angie had said she'd found it hard to continue with a heavy show schedule. She had also said that she had regrets—regrets that she'd never taken Sparkles, or herself, as far as she thought they could go. Seeing Stevie, who she knew was still in the thick of Pony Club and competition, had brought it all back.

"Anyway, she still rides for pleasure, so that proves she hasn't gone completely nuts," Stevie concluded.

At that moment, Mrs. Reg poked her head into the room. "We know!" Carole cried. "And we're about to start on the—the—" She cast her eye around for some tack that looked like it needed cleaning.

Mrs. Reg chuckled. "Would you believe that for once I didn't come in here to tell you girls to get to work?"

All three Saddle Club members shook their heads emphatically. "Absolutely not," Stevie said. "Unless something strange happened in the three days I was gone."

"Well, all right—you win. If you want, you can sweep the floor in here and rake the aisle, but otherwise, my daughter-in-law is waiting outside to take you to visit a certain colt," Mrs. Reg informed them.

Calling back promises to do double duty the following afternoon, Carole, Lisa, and Stevie raced to the driveway and jumped into Deborah's car. Deborah whizzed along the winding back roads of Willow Creek, and in no time at all they were pulling into the Grovers' driveway. "Hey, isn't that Samson?" Carole asked, pointing to the horse Mr. Grover was working with in the outdoor ring.

"It sure is. Let's go say hi," said Lisa. The girls were thrilled that they had happened to arrive in the middle of one of Samson's lessons.

Samson was fully tacked up in a saddle and a bridle with a lunging cavesson over it. The stirrups were hanging down at his sides. Mr. Grover stood in the middle of the ring as if he were lunging the colt, but without a lunge line. As the girls approached he asked Samson to "ho-ho," and the colt stopped quietly. "Good boy, good boy," Mr. Grover told him.

Stevie looked pleasantly surprised, but Carole and Lisa were flabbergasted. They ran over to greet the pair, with Deborah in tow.

Mr. Grover clipped a lead line onto Samson's bit and led him to the rail. "Glad you could make it. We're just about done for the day, so you can take him in and untack him if you want."

Normally the girls would have jumped at the chance. But first they peppered Mr. Grover with questions to learn what he had done to make Samson adjust to the stirrups so quickly.

"You girls did the most important part," the trainer said. "You made him into a lovely horse who likes people. I didn't do anything special. Let's see . . . first I lunged him. He was pretty excited to begin with, so I let him play all he wanted just as long as he kept moving. It didn't take too long for him to get bored of all his fussing. After he settled down, I took the lunge line off and I've been free-lunging him. That way he feels like he's in charge. Thanks to you three, he knows his voice commands perfectly. Don't you, boy?" Mr. Grover gave Samson a good pat. Then he handed the lead line to the girls and went to say hello to Deborah.

"Why didn't we think to lunge him?" Stevie whispered.

"Or to *let* him play until he got over it?" Lisa asked.

Carole watched Mr. Grover walk toward Deborah. Like his personality, his walk was energetic and steady—two incredibly important qualities in a horse trainer. "It sounds so simple when he explains it, but it's more than what Mr. Grover said. There's a way about him—maybe because he's older or has so much experience—that would make any horse respect him and trust him. I guess that's what it means to be a real professional."

Lisa and Stevie could see Carole's mind beginning to wander to her dreams about her future as a trainer or professional rider. They were about to say something when Samson brought Carole back down to earth with a playful butt of his nose.

"I guess we should take you in, huh?" Carole said, rubbing the velvety forehead. The three of them turned happily to lead Samson to the Grovers' barn. Already the visit had confirmed that the separation from the colt was going to be worthwhile.

"Letting go can be hard, but sometimes it's the only thing you *can* do," Lisa remarked.

Carole gave her a curious look. "Say, Lisa?"

"Yeah?"

"Do you realize what you just did?"

Lisa shook her head.

"You just figured out the point of Mrs. Reg's story!" Carole exclaimed.

"Wait a minute," Stevie spoke up, "Do you mean to tell me Mrs. Reg's been telling her incomprehensible stories while I've been gone?"

"Only one," Carole replied. "And it was all about how her Max, Max the Second, went off and studied architecture and didn't want to run Pine Hollow at first."

"Huh?" said Stevie.

Carole smiled. "That's what we said. But now it makes sense. The point was that people—and horses—will eventually do what they're meant to do. It's just that sometimes they need to get their way—or their head—first."

"You're right. It does make sense now. And you know what? Samson's going to be more than a good pleasure horse when Mr. Grover's finished training him," Lisa said confidently. "He's going to be *pure* pleasure."

The girls laughed. "Even though I'm happy he's here, I can't wait till he comes home," Carole confessed.

128

"Come home?" Stevie repeated, realizing something. "That means he'll have a homecoming."

"And?" Lisa asked.

"And you know what *that* means!"

"What?" Carole asked.

"That we'll have to throw him a welcome-home party!" Stevie replied.

Lisa and Carole had a short, whispered consultation. "We've decided to let you plan the party," Carole announced after a minute. Lisa nodded.

"After all," the two of them said in unison, "you *are* the expert!"

ABOUT THE AUTHOR

BONNIE BRYANT is the author of many books for young readers, including novelizations of movie hits such as *Teenage Mutant Ninja Turtles* and *Honey, I Blew Up the Kid*, written under her married name, B. B. Hiller.

Ms. Bryant began writing The Saddle Club in 1986. Although she had done some riding before that, she intensified her studies then, and found herself learning right along with her characters Stevie, Carole, and Lisa. She claims that they are all much better riders than she is.

Ms. Bryant was born and raised in New York City. She still lives there, in Greenwich Village, with her two sons.

Don't miss Bonnie Bryant's next exciting
Saddle Club adventure . . .

RIDING CLASS
The Saddle Club #52

Emily has cerebral palsy, but she and her specially
trained horse get around just fine. The Saddle Club
girls make friends with Emily and take her on her first
trail ride.

Unfortunately, Emily's wonderful outing at Pine
Hollow Stables is marred by someone who doesn't
think disabled people belong there. Veronica
diAngelo is the most unbearable snob ever! The Saddle Club and Emily cook up a plan to show Veronica
what real riding class is.